"Woohoo!" Jen grab[...] [...] tight. "Do you believ[...]

Jesse shook his h[...] [...] Duets scored free furniture for us, or the fact that I am standing here holding an incredibly gorgeous naked brunette in my arms?"

Jen kissed him playfully on the nose. "Either-or," she teased. Then she looked into his eyes. "Can we go shopping today?" she pleaded, sounding very much like a little girl begging to go to a toy store.

"I have to do a little work for the marketing department. Maybe you should go ahead and pick out at least some of the furniture on your own."

Jen shook her head. "No way, Jesse. This is *our* apartment now, remember. Not yours, or mine . . . *ours*."

Check out these other books from Simon Pulse!

Nancy Krulik

NEWLY WED

Simon Pulse
New York London Toronto Sydney

〰〰SIMON PULSE
An imprint of Simon & Schuster
Children's Publishing Division
1230 Avenue of the Americas, New York, NY 10020

Copyright © 2005 by Nancy Krulik

SIMON PULSE and colophon are registered trademarks of Simon & Schuster, Inc.

Designed by Ann Zeak
The text of this book was set in Adobe Caslon.

Manufactured in the United States of America
First Simon Pulse edition January 2005
10 9 8 7 6 5 4 3 2 1

Library of Congress Control Number 2004106718
ISBN 0-689-87660-2

For Danny, naturally.

Contents

NEWLY
WED

I Do . . . Don't I?

I'm getting married today.

I'm going to promise to love this man for as long as I live, in front of everyone I've ever known.

From then on, I'm going to be sombody's wife.

I've never been so scared of anything.
—Jen

Jennifer Barnes sat in front of her laptop and stared at the words on the screen. They looked strange to her. Almost like she'd spelled them wrong or something. But that wasn't it. It was just that today, nothing seemed to be normal.

Only yesterday, at her rehearsal dinner, Jen

had been so sure about everything. But now, sitting here all alone in the bride's room in the back of the church, just minutes away from becoming Mrs. Jennifer Merriman, wife of Mr. Jesse Merriman, Jen wasn't certain of *anything*—except maybe the fact that she was going to be sick.

It wasn't that Jen didn't love Jesse. She did. It was just that this was all happening so fast. She and Jesse had only met eight months ago. How much could you actually know about a person in just eight months?

Jen smiled ruefully. Wouldn't her mother love to know what she was thinking right now? That was the exact same argument she'd given Jen when Jen and Jesse had told her that they were engaged. In fact, her mother's words were ringing in her ears over and over again as she sat and stared at the computer screen.

"Are you crazy?" her mother had shouted at her. "You barely know this guy. You met him over the Internet on that crazy computer of yours. He could be anybody! A murderer. A thief. A married man! What do you really know about him, Jennifer?"

As usual, her mother's reaction had been

completely over the top. Sure, Jen had met Jesse on the Internet—everyone did these days. They'd both submitted profiles to the Duets Dating Service. But that was just how they met. It wasn't like they'd never gotten together in person. This wasn't some weird relationship like you'd see on an episode of *Ricki Lake*—"I Want to Meet My Online Lover in the Flesh!" She and Jesse were a real-life item. Their relationship was no different than any other couple's.

Still, there was a grain of truth to what her mother had said. What did she really know about Jesse? What did *anyone* know about the person they were going to marry? It was all sort of a gamble.

Well, there was *one* thing Jen knew. Jesse made her laugh. He always had, even before they'd actually met in person. Jen had to smile as she thought about the first time she'd seen Jesse's personal ad on the Duets Web site. She could still remember every word.

Business Major Looking for a Merger
There's a debit in my heart. I'm looking for the girl who can make things add up. If you like doing crossword puzzles on rainy Sundays, spending lazy autumn afternoons walking on the

beach, and watching scary movie marathons (popcorn a must!), then you might be the missing X in my equation.

At the time, Jen had thought it was such a cute ad. Funny and clever. Unique. The ad was also kind of corny, even goofy. And maybe just a *little* uptight. Which, she recalled with a slight grin, were the exact words she would use to describe Jesse.

Jesse Merriman wasn't anything like the guys Jen had dated before. For one thing, Jesse had a life plan. An actual map of where he was heading, and where he wanted to wind up—both personally and professionally. The guys Jen had known before him had needed a map just to get them from their dorm room to the student center at the University of New Jersey. But that was the way Jen's fellow art and philosophy students were.

Jesse, on the other hand, was no art student. He was all business—accounting, to be exact. Numbers were his thing. All kinds of numbers— dollars and cents, speed limits, minutes on a watch. Jesse had at least *five* watches. One of them even showed the time in different time zones all over the world! Why Jesse needed to know what time it was in Zimbabwe was something Jen knew she would never understand. But Jesse was into exactness. From his thick longish blond hair, which he was fanatical about combing until not one single strand was out of place, to his Nike Shox, with the bows tied at exactly the same size.

Thinking back on it, maybe Jesse's practicality and exactness was what had attracted Jen to him in the first place. He was so different from her. So different from anyone in her world. While the guys she knew would take her to dive bars with names like Dirty Frank's or McSulley's, Jesse took her on actual outings—like last October when he'd planned that romantic getaway at the inn in Connecticut. He'd actually rented two bikes, and they'd followed a trail to a pumpkin patch. It would have been the perfect afternoon, had it not started raining halfway back to the inn. Even a control freak like Jesse couldn't control the weather after all. And riding back to the inn through the thick mud trails had been murder.

Of course *she* had planned a few good outings herself, like the time this past spring when she convinced Jesse to drive to Philadelphia to check out the Barnes Museum and to Pat's for dinner, where she ordered cheese fries, and he had a cheesesteak. He hadn't exactly liked getting the grease from the meat all over his shirt, and he'd yawned a few times during the tour of the art exhibit, but she was pretty sure he'd had a good time.

She laughed. People said that opposites attract. She and Jesse definitely had that going for them.

Jen shook her head. No, that wasn't it. She knew exactly what had first attracted her to Jesse. It was his butt. Jesse had the most incredible tush. Tight. Muscular. He looked so damned good in jeans. She would never forget the first time she'd seen him walking away from her. He'd had to leave the coffeeshop, where they'd arranged to meet, to put a few quarters in the parking meter. She'd watched him as he walked out the door, wondering just how that tight tush might look without any clothes on. From that moment on, she was hooked.

But were a great set of buns a good enough reason to spend the rest of your life with someone?

"You look like a cupcake covered in frosting!" Jen's best friend, Careen, interrupted her thoughts as she came prancing into the bride's room.

Jen looked down at the lacey white dress with the puffy sleeves and princess neckline she was wearing and sighed. "Duets," she said simply.

Careen nodded understandingly. "It's the price you pay for a free wedding."

Jen couldn't argue with that. Ever since she and Jesse had won the "Just Duet" wedding contest (for the yummiest couple of the year who hooked up through their site), all the costs of their nuptials were being picked up by the dating service. The Duets site was doing everything for them: picking out their clothing, choosing the menu, creating the floral arrangements, even buying the wedding cake. All Jesse and Jen had to do was show up . . . *and promise to chronicle their first year of marriage on the Duets Web site*. It was all part of a promotional campaign to show that true romance really could be found online.

Jen and Jesse had gone back and forth about whether or not to enter the contest. After all, they knew that they would have to be completely honest with Duets—and that their friends and family (not to mention any strangers who decided to check out the site) would get the inside scoop on *everything* they were up to.

But in the end, it was an offer Jesse and Jen couldn't refuse—considering how broke they were. Jen's parents had refused to pay for the wedding. They wanted Jen to graduate from college before she got married. And Jesse's parents hadn't coughed up any cash either— they weren't exactly thrilled that one of their male heirs was marrying a girl who was majoring in art history and minoring in philosophy. They were looking for someone a bit more professional to fit into the family fold. Someone a little more stable and uptight. Sort of like Jesse's mother.

"What is she going to do with that kind of degree?" Adele Merriman had asked her son when Jesse had first told his parents about Jen. Jesse hadn't exactly been able to answer her.

At the time, Jen and Jesse had laughed about their parents' objections. They couldn't believe how closed-minded the older generation could be. They felt like a modern-age renegade Romeo and Juliet. It was all very romantic.

But for a while there it seemed as though their parents might have the last laugh. After all, there was no way Jen and Jesse could afford to pay for a wedding. Jesse had just started his first job in the business department of an appliance manufacturing company. And Jen was about to enter her senior year in college, with no real career plans. The only money she had was some spare cash she made by selling her homemade jewelry at flea markets. Between them, Jen and Jesse didn't even have enough money for a flight to Las Vegas for one of those quickie Britney-type weddings—without the annulment part, of course.

Which was why they'd finally decided to enter the contest. What was the big deal anyway? As Jen had pointed out to Jesse, everyone was baring their soul to the world these days. Reality shows were full of people who went into "confessionals" and described their feelings, after having their day to day lives taped, edited, and put on the air. And *they* had no control over what the audience saw and heard. At least she and Jesse could control what went on the Duets site. Jesse couldn't argue with that. He was all about control.

But what had really gotten Jesse to agree to enter the contest was the fact that Jen had found the thought of having their innermost secrets broadcast to the world a total turn on. Up until then, he'd never realized what an exhibitionist his future bride could be. But Jen had been glad to show him, and to turn him on to the many uses of a video camera.

Jen smiled, recalling how they'd been so excited when they'd found out they'd be chosen as the winning couple in Duets' wedding promotion. Wow! A fully paid wedding with all the bells and whistles. The contest prize was a very sweet deal—at least that's what Jesse and Jen had thought at first. They didn't even have to do anything! But then it became clear that Duets insisted on doing everything *their* way. The wedding they'd created had nothing to do with who Jen and Jesse (or J-squared, as Careen liked to call them) really were. Instead, it was Duets's idea of a storybook wedding—the kind they thought the users of their service might want to have.

Which explained how Jen had wound up in the lacey white monstrosity she was currently wearing. "You really think this dress is that bad?" she asked Careen nervously.

"No," Careen answered far too quickly.

Jen shot her a look.

"Okay. So, maybe it's a little froufrou for you," Careen admitted.

Jen yanked at one of the bows on her sleeves. "A little?"

Careen giggled. "It's just that I can't believe you're wearing white. I mean, *come on*. White's so . . . so . . ."

"So *virginal*?" Jen filled in the blank.

"Which isn't exactly you," Careen agreed.

"You either," she reminded her.

"Hey, I'm not the one in the white cupcake dress," Careen shot back.

Jen laughed for the first time all day. "Well, at least *I'm* not in baby blue satin." She rolled her eyes.

Careen looked down. Her petite, thin frame was too small for the yards of blue shimmery fabric that had been wrapped around her. She was nearly drowning in the dress. "I'm a *very* good friend for wearing this," she teased.

"Sorry about the dress," Jen told her sincerely. "I really didn't have any say."

"I know. Don't sweat it. Besides, I'm wearing black silk underwear and a red garter underneath. Duets can't control everything, you know."

Jen laughed. "You'll never change, Careen."

"Hey, you never can tell who you might meet at one of these shindigs. My dream guy might be sitting in that church right now. I just want to be prepared."

"Well, there's always Artie. . . ."

"Oh crap," Careen looked like she was going to be sick. "That pompous jerk? Hell, I need to carry a dictionary around just to know what he's talking about half the time. Those SAT words are so obnoxious."

"I'm with ya," Jen assured her. She frowned slightly. "My fiancé has the worst taste in best friends."

"Luckily, you don't," Careen joked.

Jen giggled. Then she grew quiet. "It's almost time," she said slowly, reaching up and sticking a few sprigs of baby's breath into the braided bun in the back of her head. She studied herself ruefully. She looked like a fairy tale princess— which was definitely not the way she'd imagined her wedding day. If she'd had her way, she and Jesse would be on the beach at the Jersey Shore, getting married barefoot in the sand. But that wasn't what Duets had had in mind.

"It's still not too late to get out of it," Careen

said. She took a seat on the loveseat beside her best friend and stared into her eyes pointedly. "But in a few minutes it *will* be."

"Thanks for the vote of confidence."

"Look, it's not that I don't like Jesse. . . ."

"You *don't* like him, Careen," Jess reminded her.

Careen sighed. "Okay. But that's not the point."

"Then what *is* the point?" Jen asked. She was getting annoyed now.

"The point *is*, this is forever. You know, *till death do you part*? Think about it, Jen. Do you really want to be a businessman's wife for the rest of your life? Don't you remember that song that Dave wrote about businessmen? Back then, you thought those lyrics were poetic genius."

Jen sighed. Dave was her ex. Careen had liked *him* a lot. Everyone in their crowd had. It was impossible not to. He was a long-haired musician with a bright smile and a quick mind. A soulful poet with amazing insights. A philosopher with a Fender ax.

Unfortunately, he was never able to keep his pecker in his pocket.

"'Businessman, businessman. Gonna step on who I can . . . ,'" Careen began chanting the chorus to one of Dave's angrier songs.

"Cut it out," Jen groaned. "You know Jesse's not like that. He's an honest guy. He cares about people. And he's smart. He doesn't have to step on people to succeed. He's going to get far because he works hard."

"Do you *hear* yourself?" Careen demanded. "'He's going to get far.' Since when do you care about things like that?"

"I don't!" Jen insisted. "But I do care about Jesse. He's a lot more than his job, Careen. He's a great guy. Funny. And incredibly romantic. He brings me boxes of chocolates just because it's Tuesday. I find little cards and gifts in my backpack, or under my pillow in the morning. He does it just to let me know he's thinking about me."

"I think I'm going to gag," Careen teased.

"And it's not just the gifts," Jen continued, pointedly ignoring Careen's sarcasm. "He's honest, and handsome, and so much fun. Everyone loves him. Someday he's going to make a great dad. I can just see him pitching baseballs in the backyard, or teaching the kids to skate."

"*Jesse* ice-skates?" Careen asked, surprised.

"See, you don't know him as well as you think you do," Jen answered triumphantly. "But I do know him. I believe in him. He'll always love me. And I'll always love him. He's the one I want to take the journey with, Care."

Jen stood there for a moment, silent. For the first time all day, the butterflies in her stomach stopped flitting around. A sense of unbelievable calm came over her.

She really did love Jesse. It was going to be okay.

"All right, then. Let's do it, " Careen replied. She picked up Jen's long white veil from the table and gently placed it on the bride's head. "Every journey begins with a single step, right? So, it's time for you to step out there and get this thing started."

"Just one last thing," Jen said. She placed her fingers on her computer keyboard and quickly deleted the last line she'd typed. Then, she quickly replaced it with:

I've never been so sure of anything.

"Man, my palms are sweaty," Jesse whispered to

his best man, Artie, as he stood at the alter waiting for the music to begin. He was feeling very warm. And he was pretty sure that it wasn't because of the hot August humidity outside. This was more like stress-heat. He wiped a piece of his straight blond hair from his forehead and began some deep breathing.

"Your breath's not so great either," Artie warned. "Got a breath strip?"

Jesse frowned. "Great. I'll go to kiss the bride and she'll run off screaming."

"If she's intelligent," Artie teased.

"Very funny." Jesse looked around at the church. There were flowers everywhere: big bouquets of lilies and white roses. *Very traditional bridal.* He knew his mother was probably happy with them. She was big on tradition. Jen, on the other hand, probably would have wanted sunflowers or daisies. Those were her favorite flowers. Nothing fancy or expensive. Just happy flowers that reminded her of the sun. As for himself, well, Jesse didn't care. Flowers didn't mean a whole lot to him. He never understood what the big deal was. Why waste money on something that's going to die soon, anyhow? In fact, Jen was always teasing him about it. She liked to say that Jesse couldn't stop to smell the roses because he had no idea what roses looked like.

The pews were filled on both sides. Jen's mom was in the front row on the right, trying to keep a smile on her face but not really succeeding. Sannah Barnes was taking the marriage of her only daughter pretty hard. Jesse was pretty sure he wasn't the problem. It was just that Mrs. Barnes worried that this marriage was yet another of Jen's flighty whims. Jesse understood that. He'd worried about that himself. But in the end, he'd decided that Jen knew what she was doing. And so did he. Together they would convince her mom of that.

Jesse's mom and dad were on the other side of the aisle. They didn't seem any more joyous than Jen's mom. In fact, Jesse's mom was downright stone-faced. Not that that was all that different from how she usually was. Adele Merriman wasn't exactly known for her effusive personality.

On both sides of the aisle, people were fidgeting in their seats, squirming around, looking toward the door in the back. But, as of yet, the bride had not emerged. A fact that was not lost on Jesse.

"We've been waiting up here a long time," Jesse murmured nervously to his best man. "What if she's changed her mind? What if she's decided not to go through with this?"

"Relax," Artie replied. "We've been standing here barely more than a nanosecond. Your betrothed will be your bride before you know it."

Artie wasn't kidding. At that very moment, the organist in the back of the church began to play "We've Only Just Begun."

"Oooh." A collective murmur went through the room as Jesse's niece and nephew, Samantha and Max, made their way down the aisle. Samantha, a chubby eight-year-old, with dark curls and a mischievous smile, sprinkled rose petals over the carpet. She seemed thrilled to have everyone staring at her. Her younger brother, on the other hand, was a very angry ring bearer. The scowling five-year-old stomped down the aisle in the tiny tuxedo and tie that the people at Duets had made him wear. As he reached the end of the aisle, Max practically threw his blue velvet pillow at his mother, Jesse's sister-in-law Meg. "Do I get my candy now?" he shouted at her.

Jesse choked back a giggle. He could tell

from the expression on Meg's face that she didn't see the moment as particularly comical. But Jesse sure did. And he was pretty certain Jen would think it was a scream when she saw it in the video.

A moment later Careen began her slow descent down the aisle. Jesse had to choke back yet another laugh as he observed his parents' reaction to the appearance of Jen's best friend. Careen, with her eggplant-purple-tinged hair, and red rose tattoo peeking out from the bustline of her dress, wasn't exactly the kind of girl the Merrimans were used to seeing at formal affairs—or anywhere else, for that matter. She was a free spirit, an artist. She just took a little getting used to.

At least that's what Jen kept telling Jesse. Frankly, he still couldn't really relate to Jen's flaky best friend. The most he could do was accept that she was going to be a fixture in their lives, and try not to let her make him too crazy.

Suddenly the music changed. Strains of "Here Comes the Bride" wafted into the room. Everyone in the audience rose and turned their attention to the doorway. Jesse looked toward the door and waited with anticipation.

And there she was.

Jesse gasped when he got his first glimpse of Jen walking down the aisle on her father's arm. She was definitely a vision in her white gown and long tulle veil. A smile rose to his lips.

Despite his best intentions, Jesse could feel his cheeks beginning to vibrate. He bit his lip hard, and dug his fingers into the palm of his hand. He didn't want to laugh. Not now. Not in the middle of his own wedding. But he just couldn't hold it in. Jen was wearing what could only be described as the most un-Jen dress he'd ever seen. It was all flouncy and poofy. Like the kind of thing they would give a bride on a bad *Saturday Night Live* skit. He shut his eyes, trying not to picture the look Jen must have had on her face when she first saw it. He began to chuckle at the thought of it.

Jen frowned slightly at Jesse's reaction to her appearance. But there was no anger in her sparkling blue eyes. Rather they were filled with amusement. She knew exactly what Jesse was thinking. They were in sync that way. As her blue eyes met his deep, dark brown ones, Jen opened her lips and let loose with some laughter of her own—a rich, bell-like giggle that came right from her soul. Jesse thought Jen's laughter was magical. Like a song.

Jesse's mother seemed paralyzed at the sound of it. But Careen was thrilled. She, too, began to laugh, letting out a long stretch of her signature loud, horsey guffaws. The laughter was contagious. Soon almost everyone on Jen's side of the aisle was giggling too. Even a few of the Merriman guests began to chuckle—although most of them weren't 100 percent sure what the joke was.

As Jen reached the end of the aisle, Jesse took her hand in his. Unlike his own nervous, sweaty palms, Jen's hand was cool, calm, and collected. She seemed happy, and sure of what they were doing. Jesse's dark brown eyes danced with joy and pride. He'd never felt luckier in his life. It seemed absolutely incredible to him that he was actually marrying this magnificent woman. Somehow this magical creature, who was able to see the humor in anything, even her own wedding, had chosen him over anyone else to share her life with. He didn't know what he had done to deserve her. But he was certainly glad. He squeezed her hand. She squeezed back.

The rest of the service was a total blur of

exchanged vows, corny organ music, and the exchanging of the rings. It was all going so fast, Jesse wasn't sure he'd remember a thing.

And then the reverend told him to kiss the bride. Holding Jen—*his wife*—in his arms was a feeling Jesse knew he would never forget. He clutched her tightly to him and kissed her hard. Jen playfully teased his lips open with her tongue, and dropped her hand until she was gripping Jesse's butt. He pulled her even closer. It was as though they'd forgotten anyone else was around.

At least until Careen hissed into their ears, "Save it for the honeymoon."

Jesse opened his eyes suddenly and looked at her with surprise. Careen grinned, knowing full well she'd just jerked the groom right back to reality. "Come on, break it up," she teased. "Let's get to the reception. I need a drink."

Well, I'm a married man. Hmmm . . . that sounds pretty good to me. Marriage feels wonderful. Also a little strange. I keep looking down at my hand to see if the gold ring is still there. I'm incredibly conscious of it. The shiny metal keeps catching my eye, and it feels really weird on my finger. Before today, I never wore any jewelry—except a watch, of course. I keep turning the band around and around, checking to make sure it hasn't fallen off.

My father can't even get his ring off his hand anymore. After twenty-seven years of marriage, it's like it's part of his finger. The skin has kind of grown around it. I wonder if that's going to happen to me?

I wonder if I'll mind.

—Jesse

Chopped Liver Swans, Cosmopolitans, and Boy George

"Ladies and gentlemen. May I present, for the first time anywhere, Mr. and Mrs. Jesse Merriman!"

The bandleader's voice rang in Jen's ears as she and Jesse swept into the ballroom to the sound of the Bill Steiner Orchestra's rendition of Madonna's eighties hit "Holiday." *Mrs. Jesse Merriman*. The name sounded strange. Also annoying. Her name wasn't Jesse, after all. It was Jennifer. Jennifer Merriman.

Okay, that sounded strange too.

Jen and Jesse hurried over to their table—a huge dais in the front of the room. The two white wicker chairs—thrones, almost—in the center of the table had been left empty for them. As they took their seats, someone—Artie, probably—began clinking a knife against the side of his glass.

Jen knew what that meant. She leaned over and placed her lips against Jesse's. He raised one eyebrow suggestively at the crowd, and then dipped her backward in a long, romantic kiss.

"Oh God, don't get them started again," Careen moaned from her seat at Jen's left.

The orchesta leader must have felt the same way, because at that very moment the group broke into a slightly off-key version of Culture Club's "I'll Tumble for Ya." Jen began to laugh, and the kiss was instantly broken.

The kiss wasn't the only thing disturbed by the music. It was obvious that Careen's mood was brought down by it as well. She made a face as the tune droned on. "Oh man, that guy's voice is awful," she complained to Jen. "Boy George must be rolling in his grave."

Artie, who was seated on Careen's other side, turned to her and shook his head. "Actually, he's still alive."

What a know-it-all, Jen and Careen thought simultaneously. When it came to Artie, they shared the same opinion.

"Well, they should at least bury this song," Careen replied, rolling her eyes. "What's with all this eighties music, anyway?"

"Duets chose the musical selections," Jesse remarked. "I don't know why they went with this stuff, though. We weren't even in kindergarten when this was popular."

"*I* know why they picked it," Artie offered.

"I knew you'd say that," Careen remarked. "Ouch," she added as Jen kicked her discreetly in the ankle. She turned to her best friend. "What was that for?"

Artie didn't seem to notice that Jen and Careen were bored with his line of conversation. He just rambled on. "I think they felt the eighties were a safe era. No seventies drug references, no nineties violence-tinged rap. No current profanity."

"No talent," Careen added ruefully as she took a big sip of her Cosmopolitan. She glanced up at the band leader, who was now attempting to do a version of the robot as he broke into the eighties cult hit "We Are Devo."

"Actually, the eighties are quite the trend right now. It's a retro-kitsch movement," Artie continued.

"You don't say," Careen replied with a droll tone to her voice.

Artie was immune to her sarcasm. "Waves of nostalgia often wash over the country when there are troubles in the world," Artie continued in his slightly condescending monotone. "It's a search for a happier time."

Suddenly the orchestra switched its beat. This time the song was more raucous and wild. Jen didn't recognize it at all. But the sound of the guitar riff sure rang a bell with Jesse and Artie.

"Hey, that's "Rock Lobster," Artie exclaimed, grabbing Jesse by the elbow. "Come on, bro. This was a big hit at the frat house, remember?" Within seconds the two former fraternity brothers were in the middle of the dance floor, sharing a little nostalgic moment of their own.

"Eighties music and Artie," Careen moaned. "Can you imagine anything worse?"

"Oh God, yes," Jen gulped. "Much worse. Here comes Mommy Dearest." She turned her eyes toward the dance floor. Her mother-in-law was cautiously making her way over to where Jen and Careen were standing.

"Hello, Jennifer," Adele Merriman said. "What a lovely dress. Those people at Duets certainly had better taste than I ever would have dreamed. It's such a lovely style for you. You look just like a princess."

Careen choked on her Cosmopolitan. She coughed so hard, the pink liquid came out her nose.

Jen tried not to join Careen in hysterics. Instead, she asked, "You remember my best friend, Careen Carlisle, don't you, Adele?"

Jesse's mother nodded. "You're the painter, right?"

Careen shrugged. "Actually, I'm more of a mixed-medium type of girl."

"Mm-hmm," Adele replied distantly. Her eyes fell toward the rose tattoo on Careen's chest and then moved to her right hand, where Careen was wearing a frightening skull-shaped ring with emerald green stones for eyes. Adele looked up and glanced nervously around the room. "Oh look, there's Carla Phelps. She's from my bridge club. I should really say hello. I'll speak to you later, Jennifer dear. It was nice seeing you again, Karen."

"That's Careen," Careen corrected her. But Adele didn't hear. She was hurrying off too quickly.

"All right, that *was* worse than Artie," Careen admitted as she handed Jen her half-finished Cosmo. "Here, you need this more than I do."

"You're not kidding," Jen agreed, downing what was left of the pink cocktail in one big gulp. She looked around at the ballroom. White paper wedding bells hung over the doorway. Each table was decorated with a small wedding cake all its own, complete with a tiny little bride and groom. And the Bill Steiner Orchestra was set up beneath a silver and white banner that read, DUETS CONGRATULATES JENNIFER AND JESSE. "Have you gotten a load of this place?" she asked her best friend.

"Duets has really done it up," Careen agreed. She squinted as a bright white light was shone directly into her eyes and a microphone was literally shoved into her face.

"Do you have anything to say to the bride, here?" the video cameraman demanded of her.

"Nothing you'd want to broadcast on that Duets Web site," Careen assured him.

"Aren't you happy for your friend?"

"Ecstatic," Careen replied drolly.

Jen gave her a strange look. "Careen?"

"Relax, sweetie. I've never been happier for you. I think J-squared is the perfect union."

"That's better," Jen said.

"After all, if it weren't for you and Jesse," Careen continued, "I might never have gotten the chance to ever hear 'Hungry Like a Wolf,' again. I think my mother listened to that one when she was pregnant with me."

The video cameraman was obviously not used to Careen's dry sort of humor. He turned quickly and walked away, shoving his microphone into the face of some other unsuspecting guest.

"Nice," Jen teased her best friend. "Thanks for all the kind sentiments."

"You know me." Careen laughed. "I'm just warm and fuzzy all over."

Jen laughed. "Well, speaking of hungry like a wolf . . ." she pointed at a brown birdlike sculpture on one of the buffet tables. "Did you see that?"

Careen wrinkled her nose. "Gross. What is it?"

"Apparently, it's supposed to be a swan," Jen told her. "At least that's what the Duets party planner has been telling people."

"What's it made of?"

Jen sighed. "Oh, that's the best part," she continued sarcastically. "It's all chopped liver. Except the eyes. Those are olives."

"It looks like it's made of baby poop," Careen told her.

Jen nodded in agreement. "And it smells even worse." She shrugged. "I guess no one mentioned to the Duets party planner that I'm a vegetarian."

"Hey, at least the bar's fully stocked," Careen assured her.

Jen smiled and looked across the room at Jesse. He and Artie were in the middle of the dance floor writhing on the ground as the band played their version of "Rock Lobster." "And I do get to go home with a pretty cute door prize," she remarked, blatantly ogling her new husband.

"Think of this whole wedding reception thing as a rite of passage to your honeymoon," Careen advised. She stopped for a moment and looked at her best friend with concern. "Please tell me Duets didn't plan that, too."

"No. They're just covering the wedding."

"Well, that's a relief. Remind me again where are you two crazy kids going?"

"Bermuda."

Careen was obviously impressed. "That must have cost a lot of bucks. How'd you get the gelt?"

"It's the off-season, so it's not that expensive," Jen explained. "And my cousin Risa gave us her discount. She's studying to be a travel agent. She booked the whole thing and got us a pretty good deal. I put it on my credit card. I figure we can pay for it later with wedding money."

"Good plan," Careen agreed. "By the way, speaking of wedding gifts, I have something really special for you and your other half. But it's not—"

Before she could finish her sentence, Artie's monotonous voice could be heard booming out from the microphone on the stage.

"As the best man, it is my honor and responsibility to make a toast to this connubial couple," he began.

"*Connubial?* Oh shit, here we go," Careen moaned. "An SAT toast. Should be fascinating."

"I'd better go stand over there next to Jesse," Jen told her best friend.

"Oh sure, leave me here with no one to goof

on Artie with," Careen complained. "Real nice."

"Come on, Care. He's toasting the bride and groom. I have to stand with Jesse. I'm the bride, he's the groom—remember?"

"Go ahead. J-squared is official now. I'll get used to it."

"Thanks for being so understanding," Jen teased as she gave Careen a peck on the cheek and hurried over to the doorway, where Jesse was standing. Oddly, he was pretty far from the best man. In fact, there was a crowd of guests between them. Artie couldn't even see Jesse. Of course, he was too self-absorbed to care.

"For those of you who don't know me, my name is Artie Samson. I'm Jesse's best friend." He paused for a moment, obviously for effect. "At least I *was* his best friend. I now pass that torch to Jennifer. I have known Jesse for five years. Not a long time, of course, but nearly an eternity compared with how long he's known his bride."

Jen flinched at that one. Artie was just giving her mother more ammunition.

"But make no mistake. Jesse did not make the decision lightly to tie the conjugal knot with Jennifer," Artie continued.

Suddenly, Jennifer heard Careen's loud

neighing laughter burst across the hall. Jennifer turned to her friend and smiled. *Conjugal knot. Oh, brother.*

"Jesse makes no decision without carefully weighing the pros and cons. Obviously Jennifer had many more pros that anyone could imagine."

"What was that supposed to mean?" Jen asked Jesse. "Should I be insulted?"

Jesse shrugged. "I don't know. I'm not even sure Artie knows what he's saying half the time. But we're all in trouble now. We'll be here all day listening to this toast. Giving Artie a microphone is a big mistake."

Sure enough, Artie was droning on and on. "Marriage has a long, distinguished history, beginning from biblical times," he continued. "And, lucky for me, so does divorce. For those of you who don't know, that's my choice of concentration in law school."

There was a touch of nervous laughter from the crowd.

"But I'm sure Jen and Jesse will never need my services," Artie continued. "They are truly soulmates who . . ."

"You think anyone would care if we snuck

out for a few minutes?" Jen whispered in Jesse's ear.

"He's my best friend. Don't you think his feelings will be hurt if we disappear during his toast?"

Jen shook her head. "He's the last one who'll notice," she assured him. "He's too busy pontificating. And, knowing Artie, he'll go on and on like this for at least thirty minutes. Come on," she pleaded. "We haven't had any time alone all day."

"Well . . . ," Jesse began unsurely. Then he looked into Jen's eyes. They were dancing mischievously. Her lips were cocked in a suggestive half smile. Mona Lisa had nothing on Jen. She could be awfully persuasive when she wanted to. "I *am* dying to get a good look at that dress," he admitted finally. "It's truly something special."

Jen frowned. "This dress. Ugh. It makes me look like a cupcake."

"Mmm. I'm hungry. Maybe I could lick the frosting off you," Jesse teased.

That did it. There was no way Jen was taking no for an answer now. She grabbed him by the arm and dragged him out of the ballroom and into the tiny bridal suite that was just off to the side. Jesse slammed the door shut with one foot, leaned his body against Jen's, and pressed her hard against the wall. "You smell so good," he murmured as he nuzzled her neck.

Jen's only response was a nibble on his earlobe.

"You're making me crazy," Jesse moaned.

"That was the idea." She took his hand and forcefully placed it on her breast.

Jesse was kissing her wildly now, pressing his lips against hers as he used his free hand to search for the zipper that was buried in the back of her dress.

But before things could go any further, the deafening sound of applause came from the nearby ballroom. "Damn!" Jesse groaned. "That was the shortest speech Artie's ever made. I guess we have to get back. It'll seem weird if they can't find us now."

Jen sighed. "Do we have to go?" she asked with disappointment. But she moved away from the wall and opened the door just the same. "Come on, let's go face the lions again."

"Wait, I just have to do one thing," Jesse told

her. He walked over to one of the two ever-present laptops Duets had provided them with, and typed a single sentence:

I CAN'T WAIT FOR THE HONEYMOON.

Let's Get Busy!

"I've done a lot of research on Bermuda," Jesse said as he reached into his carry-on bag and pulled out three large books on the subject. "We can rent mopeds and tour the island ourselves, or take guided tours of some of the beaches and local sites." He flipped through the pages of one of the books, stopping at a page that had been marked with a yellow sticky tag. "Here's a coupon for a glass-bottom boat ride. That sounds like fun, doesn't it?"

Jen leaned back in her seat and took a sip of the Bloody Mary the flight attendant had mixed for her. "I was thinking maybe we could just sort of relax. You know, find a quiet little sand dune somewhere and hang out, just the two of us."

Jesse nodded. "I've left plenty of time in the schedule for that," he assured her.

"The *schedule*?" Jen asked suspiciously.

"Well, not a schedule, exactly," Jesse replied sheepishly. "Just sort of a rough guide to each day's activities. I thought it would help make sure we got everything in."

"Jesse, this is a honeymoon, not a board meeting," Jen teased. "We don't need an agenda." She reached over and grabbed the guidebook from his hands. "Forget the books. Get rid of the sticky tags and the schedules. We've got you, me, and this adorable little string bikini I bought just for this trip. What more could we ask for?"

It was hard for Jesse to argue with logic like that. Still, he didn't think he'd be able to spend a whole week just lounging on the beach. He wasn't that kind of guy. Relaxing wasn't something he did well. He liked to keep moving. He always liked to be doing something. Which was why, as Jen closed her eyes and tried to nap, he pulled out his laptop and placed it on the tray table in front of him.

Might as well get a new message to Duets, he thought as he turned the computer on.

♥

We're on our way to Bermuda now. The seats are cramped, the food's lousy, and we've hit a bit of turbulence along the way. But I couldn't care less. I'm just so glad the whole wedding-pressure thing's over. It's going to be smooth sailing from here on out.

Funny thing, the stress didn't seem to get to Jen at all. Me, I was a walking mess—sweaty palms, stinking pits, nervous stomach. But she was like a walking vision of calm. Nothing bothered her. Not the goofy dress, the veil, the tacky music, or even the chopped-liver swan. Okay, maybe the swan bugged her a little bit. But still, I think Jen held up a lot better than I did yesterday.

Of course, when it came to our wedding night, I had no stress at all. That hotel room Duets gave us really rocked! When it comes to sex, Jen and I are totally in sync. (Not to mention, in the shower, on the floor, and on the terrace.)

I can't believe we've got a whole week alone together. No school for Jen, no work deadlines for me, no Careen, no Artie, no disapproving mothers. Just Jen and me in paradise. It doesn't get better than that.

We'll keep you posted!

—Jesse

"I can't believe it's raining," Jesse moaned as their taxi pulled up in front of the hotel. "Whoever heard of rain in Bermuda?"

"Well, Risa did say it was the beginning of the off-season," Jen reminded him. "Besides, it's just a little shower. The sun'll probably be out in no time."

Jesse looked out the car window. The rain was splashing against the car so hard, it seemed like the roof of the taxi might cave in. And the way those trees were blowing, it was like they'd topple over any minute. *A little shower? More like a monsoon.* He began to laugh.

"What's so funny?"

"You are," he said as he gave her a little peck on the nose. "Talk about seeing the glass as half full."

"Actually, I'm seeing it as completely full," Jen assured him, throwing her arms around his shoulders and kissing him strongly on the mouth. Jesse kissed her back with equal intensity.

"Ahem." The driver cleared his throat as he stopped his taxi at the entrance of a large, sprawling white building on the beach. "We're here."

Jesse pulled away from Jen's embrace and paid the man. As he opened the door and circled round to the trunk of the car, where their luggage was placed, he could hear the driver murmur something about "those damn honeymooners."

The hotel lobby was beautifully decorated. It was painted a crisp white with just the smallest touch of pale blue trim. Huge white ceiling fans circled above, and beautiful native island flowers seemed to be everywhere. Jesse could tell by the expression on her face that Jen had never seen anything so impressive. When he'd been a kid, Jesse's family had been big travelers—they'd spent winters in the Caribbean, and summers taking trips to the major cities in Europe. Nothing fancy or expensive, but traveling just the same. Jesse's folks felt that the only way to really learn about the world was to see it firsthand. In fact, in some ways it seemed like their central New Jersey house was merely a home base from which to launch their travels.

But the Barnes clan were Jersey folks through and through. Jen's family's idea of the perfect vacation was to rent a huge house in Margate or Ocean City for a couple of weeks in the summer, and spend their time going on amusement park rides and eating brunches at the Atlantic City casinos. This was the first time Jen had been out of the country.

"Amazing," she murmured, walking over to the large lobby window that overlooked the beach. "Funny, it's the same Atlantic Ocean as at home. But it looks so much bluer here. And Jesse, check it out. The sand really is pink. I thought that was just a myth!"

"Uh-oh," he replied. "I think you've been bitten."

Jen looked down at her bare arms and legs. "Bitten? By what? Do they have mosquitoes here?"

Jesse grinned. "No. I mean you've been bitten by the travel bug. It's going to be hard to keep you in New Jersey from now on."

"Oh, don't worry," Jen assured him. "I'll always be the Jersey Girl you married."

"I know. New Jersey will always be home," Jesse told her.

Jen shook her head. "Not anymore."

"What are you talking about?" Jesse gulped. He hoped Jen wasn't suddenly going to suggest that they move to Bermuda or something. It would be like her to want to do something just that crazy and spontaneous.

"I mean that now, home is wherever *you* are," Jen explained. She rubbed his arm gently.

His arm tingled under her touch. "Let's get to the room, okay?"

Jen nodded. "Don't we have to get the key first?" she giggled heading over to the register.

Jesse followed behind her. As the reached the guest registry desk, he took her hand in his. "I'm Jesse Merriman, and this is my *wife*, Jen," he said proudly.

The man behind the desk smiled. "Are you part of the podiatrist group?" he asked them.

Jen looked at him strangely. "I beg your pardon?"

"The podiatrist convention," the man explained. "Are you with that group?"

Jesse shook his head. "We're on our honeymoon," he explained.

"Oh, I apologize. Most of the hotel has been reserved for podiatrists, so I just naturally assumed . . ." He smiled kindly at Jen and Jesse as he punched a few keys on his computer. "But now I can see you two have that just-married glow. Ah, here you are. Jesse and Jennifer Merriman. You're in Room 302."

"Three zero two," Jen repeated. "I just want to remember that . . . for always."

Jesse smiled and gave her hand a squeeze. "Does the room have an ocean view?" he asked.

"No sir. But you can see the bay from the terrace," the hotel clerk replied.

"Aren't you going to carry me over the threshold?" Jen asked as she stood defiantly in front of the open door that led to their hotel room.

"Here too?" Jesse asked her. "You made me carry you over the threshold at the airport hotel last night, remember?"

"Are you saying I'm too much of a burden to carry?" Jen teased.

"Never!" Jesse declared. He swept her up and swung her over his shoulder like a sack of potatoes, giving her a close-up view of the small of his back.

"Real romantic." Jen laughed. "This isn't exactly the position I had in mind."

"You're the one who's always into new positions," Jesse reminded her, jokingly. He stopped for a minute and looked around. "Uh-oh."

"What?" Jen said, craning her neck to see the room.

"Take a look," Jesse said, tossing her down on the small day couch in the room. "Your wacky cousin booked us a room with two double beds instead of a king! Who ever heard of honeymooners sleeping in separate beds? What kind of travel agent is she, anyway?"

"She's not exactly a travel agent. At least not yet. We were sort of a practice run. She booked this trip as a project for her class."

Jesse rolled his eyes. "Well, I'll bet she doesn't get an A. " He sniffed at the air. "Do you smell something fishy?"

Jen nodded. "We're on an island. Maybe it's coming from the bay." She walked over, opened the drapes, and opened the sliding door that led to the terrace. Instantly, the smell became stronger. "Uh-oh," she said quietly.

"Uh-oh *what*?"

"Well, it's the view," Jen said.

"What, it's not of the bay?"

"It's sort of of the bay," she told him. "If you

turn your head all the way to the right and lean over the railing, you can see the water."

"What do you see if you don't lean over?" Jesse asked.

Jen gulped. He was starting to sound angry. "Now Jesse, remember, this is our paradise, no matter what. . . ."

"Oh man. I'm going to kill Risa!" Jesse declared as he stepped out to join Jen on the terrace. He looked down. "We've got a view of the *kitchen*!"

"Well, at least we'll know what's on the menu before anyone else will," Jen said meekly.

"Cute," Jesse replied in a tone that let her know he was not amused. "I should have known something would go wrong. When your kooky cousin was able to book a trip as cheaply as she did . . . well, here's a lesson: You don't get anything for nothing."

"I'm sure it was just a mistake," Jen assured him. "Why don't you call down to the front desk and see if there's another room we can have?"

Jesse's face perked up slightly. "Good idea," he told her. "It's the off-season. There must be a whole lot of rooms empty." He reached for the phone. "Hello, this is Jesse Merriman in Room 302. My *wife* and I were just wondering . . ."

Jen smiled as he explained their problem to the clerk at the desk. *Wife.* She really loved the sound of that word. Jesse had been using it all day—at the airport, on the plane, at the hotel desk. Of course, she'd been getting a real kick out of calling him her *husband,* too. It was sort of like they were two little kids playing house—only it was better, because they got to play doctor, too!

"Oh, I see," Jen heard Jesse say into the receiver. His voice no longer sounded so cheerful. "Well, of course I understand. Yes, that would be nice. Thank you. Okay."

"So?" Jen said as Jesse hung up the phone. "Should you be getting ready to lift me over another threshold?"

"Not this trip," Jesse replied. "It seems that every room in the hotel is booked. There are lots of podiatrists in Bermuda today."

"Good thing I got my toenails painted," Jen joked, trying to lift his mood. "These guys are sure to be staring at my feet."

But Jesse wasn't amused. "A honeymoon with double beds. This is a nightmare."

"Actually, it's a dream come true," Jen said with a smile.

"Huh?"

"Two beds are better than one," she explained playfully. "We can mess one up in the afternoon, and still have a set of fresh sheets to roll around on at night."

Jesse stared at her. "You're amazing," he said. "I've never known anyone who could look at things the way you do."

"We can have a good time anywhere, Jesse. All we need is us."

"I guess you're right," he agreed. "And at least the rain's stopped. Now we can rent some mopeds like I'd planned. I thought we could ride into Hamilton and shop. . . ."

"Oh no, buster," Jen contradicted him. "We're on *my* schedule now. I'm the one giving the tour. And the first stop is the bed nearest the window." She whipped off her T-shirt and unhooked her lacy lavender bra. "You don't need a moped, sweetie," she assured him as she walked over and quickly unbuttoned his shirt. She pulled him close against her and rubbed her bare skin against his. The effect was electric, a current running simultaneously through both of their bodies. Jen threw her new husband onto the bed and fumbled wildly at the buttons on his jeans. "I'm about to take you on the ride of your life."

Well, I think I finally figured out how to get my husband to relax. All it takes is a couple of Rum Swizzles and a nice massage. Of course, pink sandy beaches and incredible sunsets don't hurt either.

Besides, I did compromise a little. We went on the glass-bottom boat trip Jesse was dying to experience, and even took mopeds into Hamilton for some shopping. I bought a few beautiful sea stones. I'm going to make some jewelry out of them. Jesse bought a clock—of course. (Hey, some things even Bermuda can't change!) Apparently Bermuda is known for their clocks and watches.

Now, we're at the airport, getting ready to leave this island paradise. :(It's time to face real life, as husband and wife. But I'm not worried. If Jesse gets too stressed at home, I've got a few secret weapons packed away in my suitcase: a vial of pink sand, a couple of packages of Rum Swizzle mix, and a pair of

white Bermuda shorts. Seeing Jesse in them
is guaranteed to drive me wild!
—XXOO,
Jen

Next Time I'm
Making Reservations

Jen walked out into the late September sunshine, blinked a few times at the sudden brightness, and stretched her body out. That had been one hell of a test, but she was pretty sure she'd done okay. Art history came easily to her. She loved studying artists and learning about what made them tick. She was a walking encyclopedia on modern art, and she didn't need much persuading to talk about what she knew. She could spend hours over coffee talking with the other people in her art history classes, debating the merits of various artists. And those debates could get really heated. Most recently, a seemingly benign discussion between Jen and some of the other art history students on the influences of people like Kandinsky and Klee on the current art scene had gotten so heated that several people had gotten up and walked out of the Student Center. One guy had even gotten so mad, he'd banged on the table and knocked his hot coffee all over himself.

Jesse had found that hysterical when Jen told him the story. He couldn't imagine anyone getting so keyed up over a discussion of dead artists. Of course, get him started on a discussion of the way the Yankees were buying themselves championships and . . .

Suddenly, Jen felt herself missing Jesse. She hadn't even been awake when he'd left that morning, which meant she hadn't seen him since the night before. It seemed like an eternity.

Jen shifted the weight of her backpack to her other shoulder. Wow. Art history books were heavy. It was all the pictures they were filled with. But that was a small price to pay for being able to sit in a classroom and learn about the masters. Jen didn't consider herself an artist. She was a just a student. *Careen* was the fine arts major. The girls often joked that someday Jen would do a doctoral thesis on the great artist Careen Carlisle. Well, at least Careen joked about it. Jen wasn't kidding. She didn't doubt it in the least. As far as she was concerned, Careen was brilliant.

In fact, at that very moment, Jen was hurrying off to meet her best friend at The Beanery, a local coffeehouse just off campus. They were planning on chowing down on über-fattening scones and lattes with whipped cream.

Hey, sometimes a girl just had to go a little wild!

Jen was especially excited to get together with Careen. The girls hadn't seen each other nearly enough since Jen and Jesse had gotten married. In fact, Jen had been back from her honeymoon nearly two months, but she and Careen had only hung out together maybe half a dozen times.

Part of that was just the fact that senior year schoolwork took up a lot of time. Jen had exams to study for, and Careen had to finish several pieces for her art observations. And then there was the fact that Jen and Jesse had a lot of family obligations: dinner at the country club with the Merrimans; a Saturday night supper here and there with Jen's parents; and, of course, the obligatory baby-sitting duty for Jesse's brother, Richie, and his wife, Meg.

But there was more to it than that. Jen had to find time to be with Careen when Jesse wasn't around. Jesse had a hard time relating to Careen. She got under his skin and rubbed him completely the wrong way. Jen found that difficult to understand. She couldn't imagine anyone feeling uncomfortable around Careen. She was so much fun to be around. To Jen's way of thinking, being around Careen was like being on a really awesome roller coaster: there were ups, downs, twists and turns, and plenty of fast motion. But all of it was fun.

Of course, if she was really forced to think about it, Jen would have to admit that Jesse was more the kind of guy who liked Dumbo and It's a Small World rather than a Space Mountain risk taker. Which, come to think about it, was exactly what Careen found most distressing about Jesse. He was just too damn safe for her taste, and Jen knew it.

Careen didn't understand Jesse's appeal for Jen, but Jen never questioned it. She felt safe around Jesse. He was her rock, her stability. It didn't matter what crazy thing Jen wanted to try—Jesse would always catch her if she fell. When she was with him, she felt all warm and fuzzy, like she was seated in front of a log-burning fireplace on a cold winter's night. He grounded her in a way that no one else had ever been able to.

Jen loved her husband *and* her best friend. So, to avoid hearing Jesse moan about Careen, or listening to Careen trash Jesse, Jen had taken to keeping them apart. Like this afternoon. It was a Friday, there were no tests the next day to worry about, and Jesse wouldn't be home from work until at least six o'clock, which gave the girls plenty of time to gossip, giggle, and basically head back in time to those days before J-squared existed. They were sure to have a lot of fun!

Still, it would be nice to hear Jesse's voice right about now. As she headed over to The Beanery, Jen pulled out her cell and hit the speed dial to Jesse's work number. He picked up the phone on the first ring.

"Jesse Merriman."

Jen felt a slight tingle going up and down her spine at the very sound of him. Somehow he always brought out the whole high school crush thing in her—which was kind of embarrassing considering she was twenty-one years old. "Hey there!" Jen said excitedly. "How's it going?"

"Don't ask."

Jen sighed. Lately that had been Jesse's response to any of her questions about his job. Not that she'd ever understood his answers to her queries before, anyway. The most she could make out was that when Jesse went to work, he spent his days figuring out probablities of profit margins on the company's products—or at least it was something like that. "Okay. Let's talk about *my* day. I think I did well on that Picasso exam. Boy, am I glad that's over. He lived a long time—and painted a lot of works. They're all dancing around in my head."

"Mm-hmm," Jesse murmured. He was obviously distracted. She could hear his fingers clicking on the computer keyboard while she spoke.

"Now I'm going over to meet Careen at The Beanery."

"Uh-huh."

Jen shook her head. He wasn't hearing her. One last question and she'd hang up the phone. "What time do you think you'll be home?"

"Huh?" Jesse began.

"Home? You know that apartment we share? Are you planning on coming back to it?

"Oh, yeah," Jesse said, suddenly hearing her. "I'm sorry, babe. Things are just a little crazed around here today. Um, I'm gonna be pretty late. Maybe like seven or eight. I have to get these profit-and-loss estimates in tonight, and the numbers aren't adding up. Just leave me a couple of slices in the fridge and I'll heat 'em up when I get home."

In the background, Jen could hear Jesse's second phone line ringing. It was the internal line—the one his boss used. By now, Jen knew what that meant. "You'd better get that," she told him. "I'll see you at home."

"'Kay. Love ya."

"Back atcha," Jen replied. But her voice didn't have the usual playful tone she used when signing off with Jesse. Something he'd said had really bothered her.

"Hey, J."

Jen turned quickly as she heard Careen's voice behind her. "Oh, hi." She glanced down at her watch, and then up at the coffeehouse in front of her. She'd managed to walk all the way to The Beanery while talking to Jesse. "You're on time," she remarked with surprise to Careen.

"Actually, we're both late," Careen said, and

laughed, bobbing her newly dyed blue-green hair up and down with each chuckle. "Which of course for us, is right on time."

"Mm-hmm." Jen's absentminded tone was a perfect echo of what Jesse's had been on the phone a few moments before.

"Hello?" Careen said. "Earth to Jennifer?"

"Oh, sorry," Jen answered.

"What's wrong?"

"It's Jesse."

"Oh, I could have told you that *he* was wrong. Dead wrong."

Jen scowled. "Very funny. No, seriously, he said the weirdest thing to me just now."

"What?"

"He told me he was going to be late, and that I should leave a few slices for him in the refrigerator for dinner."

Careen looked at her strangely. "Far be it from me to defend your corporate honcho hubby, but what's wrong with that?"

"Well, what makes him think I'm ordering in pizza for dinner? Maybe I was planning on cooking something special."

Careen let out her horsey guffaw. "Yeah. Right."

"What's that supposed to mean?"

"Nothing. Except it's not like you're exactly a domestic diva, you know," Careen defended herself. "You've been married what, two months already?"

Jen nodded.

"And have you ever once cooked anything?"

Jen put her hands on her hips. "Hey, I made him scrambled eggs for breakfast last Saturday. I made spaghetti with tomato sauce last week . . ."

"You made sauce?" Careen seemed genuinely impressed.

"Well, it was from a jar," Jen admitted. "I just poured it onto the spaghetti. And I'm always making vegetable noodle soup—from the package, of course, but hey, at least. . ." She stopped mid-sentence. That was the end of her recipe repertoire. "All right, so I haven't exactly been providing homemade meals. But I've been busy. And no one said Jesse couldn't cook something." She was defensive suddenly.

"I'm not arguing with you," Careen told her. "Hey, I still eat at the dorms. I'm just saying that Jesse was making an educated guess as to what was for dinner," Careen assured her friend. "Chances are you were planning on pizza or Chinese takeout."

"Not anymore," Jen told her defiantly. "I'm cooking tonight."

Careen began to laugh. "Good one."

"No. I'm serious. I'm making dinner. A real dinner. From scratch."

"But you've never cooked anything in your life."

"Well I'm going to start now."

Careen looked at her curiously. "Where's this coming from? What's with the sudden Becky Home-ecky thing?"

Jen shrugged. "I don't know. It's not just for Jesse. I'm half of a mini-family. But our apartment doesn't feel like a family home. It's sort of a halfway house after the dorms, you know. I kind of like the idea of food cooking on the stove and delicious smells wafting through the apartment. "

Careen shook her head. "I've seen your apartment. It'll take a lot more than the smell of food to make that place feel like a real home. You've got all that junky furniture from Jesse's old place in there."

"I know, it's kind of a dump. But cooking

once in a while would be a start at making the place more homey."

"You've never cooked anything," Careen reminded her again.

Jen shrugged. "Come on. How hard can it be? All I have to do is buy one of those women's magazines at the supermarket and follow their recipes."

"This I've got to see," Careen snickered.

"Oh, you'll do more than see," Jen told her. "You're cooking with me."

"Me?" Careen's voice scaled up nervously. "Why should I make dinner for Jesse?"

"Hey, someday you may actually get married. And you might want to surprise your honey with a homemade meal. Think of this as a sort of starter class," Jen reasoned.

Careen shook her head. "Any guy I marry is going to cook for *me*."

"Okay," Jen said. "How about if I get on my knees and plead for your help?" She dropped to her knees in a scene of mock-pleading.

"Oh God, get up," Careen moaned. "I've got enough of a reputation as a drama queen."

"I owe you," Jen vowed as she stood up.

"I'll add it to the list," Careen told her. "And

just remember. If you ever tell anyone that I did this, I'll deny it."

"Hey, do you know what chives look like?" Jen asked Careen as the girls stood in the produce section of the local supermarket. "There are all these weird herbs, and I haven't a clue which is which. The labels the grocer put over the piles aren't very clear. I can't tell what they refer to."

"Why don't you buy the bottled dried stuff?" Careen suggested. "You just shake them right out of the top—like salt."

"The recipe calls for *fresh* chives," Jen pointed out. "You can't have a stir-fry with sprinkled dry chives."

"Who says?" Careen replied. "What, are there rules now?"

"I'm just trying to make it right," Jen told her. She looked so sad, it was possible she might cry.

"Okay, since we obviously don't know what we're doing, we're going to have to make some adjustments," Careen said, taking charge. "I saw this on TV. Instead of cutting up all the vegetables and spicing them up ourselves, let's use this frozen-vegetable package." She yanked a bag of vegetables out of a nearby freezer. "It's got everything that recipe calls for: onions, cauliflower, broccoli, carrots, and Asian spices. It's fool-proof, and Jesse will never know the difference."

"You think?" Jen asked.

"I *know*," Careen assured her. "He's not used to your cooking anything. He'll be so excited, he won't know *what* hit him."

"That's true," Jen admitted.

"Good. Now let's get out of here, and start the cooking. Did you get the wine?"

"The recipe doesn't call for wine."

Careen shook her head and sighed. "The wine's for me. I'm going to need it before this evening's through."

"Okay, so what do we do first?" Jen asked after unloading all her ingredients and pulling out the brand-new huge metal fry pan her aunt Roz had given her as a wedding gift.

Careen sank into the large, well-worn burgundy lounge chair in the living room. Actually, the living room and the kitchen were one room. The kitchen was just a small stove-oven combination and a refrigerator with a few cabinets overhead. "I say we start with the wine." Careen wriggled around for a few minutes, trying to get comfortable. "I can feel the springs in this thing," she moaned. "Haven't you been able to convince Jesse to get rid of his ugly furniture yet?"

Jen shook her head. "He's never going to part with his beloved chair." She sighed. "Or that hideous, seashell-shaped table," she added as she took the corkscrew from the kitchen drawer and opened the wine. "I think he likes the look of pink and white plastic, shimmering under fluorescent light."

"Too bad we can't just start a bonfire and get rid of all his junk. You could make this place look really amazing if you were able to decorate it any way you wanted."

"Yeah, well, that's not happening," Jen replied. "Although, I *was* thinking that if I could get some really funky bookshelves, and a little love seat for under the window, this place would be a lot less cluttered."

Careen took her glass of chardonnay and walked around the room. "The place would be a lot less crowded if we could get rid of these hideous things." She picked up a creamy pink, white, and blue ceramic sculpture of a ballerina with exaggerated long legs. "Lladró statues." She harrumphed. "Too Home Shopping Network for my taste . . . for *anyone* with taste."

"I know," Jen agreed. "It kills me to have to look at them every day. But the ballerina was a gift from Richie and Perfect Meg. And those other two were from members of Adele's bridge club. Jesse'd never let me get rid of them."

"Well, we could . . . ," Careen began, lifting the statue over her head and pretending to drop it.

"Careen, cut it out," Jen pleaded. "Jesse'll kill you. And that's merciful compared to what he'd do to me."

"Why? What would he do?"

Jen took a sip of her wine. "He'd make me nuts, telling me how it could never have been an accident, because Freud says there are no accidents." She laughed. "I think that's all he remembers from that one psych course he was required to take."

"Prince Charming has flaws?" Careen asked with mock surprise. "Do tell me more."

"That's it," Jen assured her. "Mostly he's the perfect husband. Which is why I want to cook this dinner for him." She glanced up at the clock on the wall. It was shaped like a cat whose tail swung back and forth, and its eyes blinked with each second. Jesse loved it. He said his grandmother had had one just like it in her kitchen when he was little. Jen couldn't bear the awful-looking thing. Its buggy eyes gave her the creeps. "He'll be home in like an hour," she said, surprised at how late it had gotten. She held up a bottle of olive oil. "I guess I'll start with this," she added, pouring the thick yellow liquid into the pan.

"You ever wonder why they label olive oil as 'virgin'?" Careen giggled as she stood and walked over to help her friend cook the meal.

"Never mind virgin," Jen added. She pointed to the label on the bottle. "This stuff's *extra* virgin."

"I wonder if that means it's never even gotten to first base," Careen mused as she poured herself another hefty glass of wine. "Poor thing. Being cooked without being kissed."

"Ouch!" Jen shouted out. She jumped up out of the way of the bubbling oil in the pan. "That stuff just leaped out the pan and burned me."

"I think it's ready for the veggies," Careen speculated.

"Don't I have to heat them first—defrost 'em or something?" Jen asked her.

Careen shrugged. "They'll cook pretty fast in that oil. Defrosting them just seems like wasted effort."

"Okay," Jen agreed. "Makes sense to me." She opened the bag with scissors and dumped the entire contents of ice-crusted veggies into the pan.

Whoosh! Within a split second a huge flame leaped up from the pan.

"Oh, my God!" Careen shouted out. "Fire!"

Jen just stood there for a moment, staring as the powerful orange flame began to paint the walls a dark charcoal black.

"Hurry! Get some water!" Careen shouted. "Pour water on it!"

Jen did as she was told. She took a cup of cold water from the sink and poured it right onto the fire. But instead of taming the flame, the water seemed to feed it, bringing the heat and brightness to an all-new high. "It's not working!" she cried out in fear as the flames swallowed the kitchen curtains in a single gulp!

Beep. Beep. Beep. The smoke detector began ringing, louder and louder. With each beep, Jen sobbed harder. She was hysterical.

Luckily, Careen was still thinking somewhat clearly—or as clearly as she could after a glass and a half of wine. She turned and spotted the small red canister beside the sink. "Is that the fire extinguisher?" she shouted anxiously over the cacophony of sobs and loud ringing. When Jen didn't—*couldn't*—answer, Careen took a chance. She grabbed the canister and pushed the button on its top. Instantly a white foamy substance shot out from the opening. It *was* a fire extinguisher. Within seconds, the flame was gone.

"Well, that's over," Careen said, falling exhausted into Jesse's chair.

Jen looked around her apartment and shook her head. It wasn't over, not by a long shot. The apartment was a *mess*. The walls were black. The curtains were gone. The tail on the cat clock had melted into a huge blob of molten plastic. And the whole place stunk of smoke. "All I wanted to do was make a nice dinner," she cried. "How did this happen?"

Before Careen could even venture a guess, there was a powerful knock at the door. "Fire Department," a strong voice boomed from the other side of the door. "Is everyone all right in there?"

Careen walked over and opened the door. Suddenly she was standing face-to-face with a beautiful example of manhood. "I think so," she said, staring into the fireman's big blue eyes. "But you're welcome to come in and check."

"We're actually required to do that, miss," the fireman told her. Careen stepped aside, and the fireman entered the apartment. He was followed by two more firefighters, all of whom were equally tall, muscular, and incredibly sexy.

"What happened here?" the firefighter with the blue eyes asked Careen.

"Ask her," Careen said, pointing to Jen. "She was the one who started it. *I'm* the one who put it out."

"Thanks a lot," Jen hissed. She blushed red. "I don't know. One minute I was pouring frozen vegetables into boiling oil, and the next minute—"

"Oil fire," a second firefighter with deep-set brown eyes and just a touch of five o'clock shadow ventured a guess.

"I tried to put it out. I poured water on the flame . . . ," Jen babbled nervously.

"You never put water on an oil fire, miss," the

blue-eyed fireman told her in a calm but firm voice. "It will only exacerbate things."

"That's *Mrs.*" Careen corrected him.

"Excuse me?"

"Her name is Mrs. Jennifer Merriman. She's married. I, however, am completely single." She smiled at the three burly firefighters. "My name's Careen. Can I get any of you gentlemen a glass of wine?"

"Actually, we're working and . . . ," the slightly unshaven firefighter began. But before he could finish his sentence, Jesse came bursting into the apartment. He was out of breath, and his face was beet red.

"Jen! Are you okay?" he shouted. He looked around the room, his eyes wild and frantic— until he spotted her.

"I'm fine," Jen assured him. She wiped a dark charcoal smudge from her forehead. "It was just a little kitchen fire."

Jesse raced over and wrapped his strong arm around Jen's small shoulders. He pulled her close, trying to protect her from the horror that could have been.

"Oil fire," the third firefighter, a muscular African American with a reassuring smile, explained to him. "It's out now. Apparently, your wife tried to extinguish it with water."

"But I managed to find your fire extinguisher," Careen said, as if to inform the firefighters of the details of her brilliant rescue. "I knew exactly what to do when the flames got high."

"Yeah, but you're also the one who told me to pour the water on the pan to begin with," Jen corrected her.

For the first time, Jesse seemed to notice that Jen's best friend was also in the room. "Careen." He gave an exasperated sigh. "I might have known this would be your fault. I can't believe you told Jen to put water on an oil fire. Everyone knows you either smother it with a lid or use a fire extinguisher."

"Well, obviously Jen and I had to learn the hard way," Careen told him firmly.

"It *wasn't* her fault," Jen told Jesse. "She was just helping me make dinner for you."

"You were doing *what*?"

"Making dinner, for *you*," Jen repeated.

"You're kidding."

Now Jen was getting a little insulted. "No. I'm not. You've been working so hard and I just thought a nice home-cooked meal . . ."

"Or, in this case, a home-cooked *home*," Careen teased.

The fireman with the five o'clock shadow let out a laugh. "Good one," he said. "I've got to share that one with the guys back at the firehouse."

Careen smiled and batted her eyes. "People do tend to like my sense of humor."

Jesse stared at Careen. He couldn't believe she was actually flirting at a time like this! "She'll do anything to meet men," he harrumphed.

Careen glared at Jesse. "That's right. This was all one big singles scheme. You know me. I'd risk my life to meet the right guy. I was just lighting a fire under my social life . . . so to speak," she barked back.

All three firefighters laughed at that one. So did Jen. It was only Jesse who refused to see any humor in the situation. "I wouldn't put anything past you, Careen," he sneered.

"Come on, Jesse. It was just an accident," Jen said in a soothing voice. She was trying to restore the peace in the room.

But Jesse would not be calmed. Now that he was certain Jen was all right, he was beginning to assess the damage to the apartment. And it was considerable. The walls were covered in smoke. The kitchen curtains were gone. He looked at his cat clock. It was a molten mess. And the fabric on his favorite chair had black smoke stains all over it. It was completely ruined. They'd have to throw it out—just like Jen had been begging him to do since they'd come home from their honeymoon. "Accident, huh?" he repeated. "Freud says there are no accidents!"

That was all it took. As Careen's and Jen's eyes met, the two began to laugh hysterically. "See, I told you," Jen blurted out between chuckles.

"You definitely know your husband," Careen agreed. She turned to Jesse. "Hey, at least those valuable Lladró statues weren't hurt. I think they look as lovely as they always have."

Her sarcasm was lost on Jesse. "Well, I'm glad for that, I guess," he agreed. Then he hugged Jen again. "More importantly, you're okay."

"It's *all* going to be okay," Jen assured him. She looked around the room. "A new coat of paint, some curtains, and a new chair—in a few days it'll be like it never happened."

Jesse took a deep breath. "I need to sit down," he gasped, as the enormity of what had happened—worse yet, what *could* have happened—suddenly hit him. He plopped down in his smoke-stained chair and bit his lip. His eyes welled up with tears. Slowly Jen went over and climbed onto his lap. She brushed back his soft, blond hair and cuddled up against his chest. They sat there for a moment in silence, huddled together for safety, suddenly unaware that anyone else was in the room.

"Well, I guess I'll be going," Careen said quietly. She turned to the firefighters. "I think your work here is done too—isn't it, fellas?"

The blue-eyed firefighter nodded. "Everything seems fine here now. The fire's out, and neither of you seem to have any smoke inhalation problems. There's nothing left for us to do but the paperwork. There are a few questions I need answered, though." He looked over at Jesse and Jen sitting in the chair.

"Oh, I can fill you in on anything you need," Careen assured him. "I'll even come back to firehouse with you if you need me to."

"That would be helpful," he said. His blue eyes looked *very* interested.

Careen picked up on his signal immediately. "Can I ride in the fire truck?" she asked suggestively.

"Sorry, uh—," he began.

"Careen."

"Sorry, Careen," he corrected himself. "That's against regulations."

Careen groaned. "I really wanted to ring your bell." She laughed. "I mean, the one on the fire truck, of course."

"Of course," Jesse said sarcastically, lifting his eyes from Jen's gaze long enough to shoot Careen a dirty look.

Careen shot him a look of her own, but said nothing as she left the apartment—followed directly by the three hot firefighters.

"She never ceases to amaze me," Jesse told Jen as they left.

"Careen *is* pretty incredible. I don't know what I would have done if she weren't here."

Jesse didn't answer. He didn't want to fight over Careen right then. He didn't want to fight at all. He was just so grateful that everything had turned out the way it had. And he wanted to make sure that nothing like this would ever happen to Jen again. "Sweetie, you've got to promise me something," he said gently.

"What?"

"Promise me you'll never cook anything again."

Jen giggled. "Oh yeah, right. Never. Not as long as we live. You're going to spend the rest of your life eating takeout and making reservations."

"I'm serious," Jesse told her. "It's not worth it. I can live on pizza, sandwiches, and Chinese takeout. But I can't live without you."

Well that totally freaked me out. Imagine getting home and finding a fire truck parked right outside your apartment building. And the closer I got to the fourth floor, the stronger that smell of smoke became. I don't think I'll be able to ever describe the feeling of panic I was experiencing as I got closer and closer to our apartment. I just know I'll never forget it.

I've never been in a situation like that before. Nothing really dangerous or bad has ever happened to me. I play it so safe that I've never even had a fender bender, or twisted my ankle playing b-ball. Jen's the risk taker. And when you take risks, sometimes you get burned. Of course, only Jen could make cooking vegetables a risk.

Hey, so I didn't marry a domestic goddess. She's a goddess in all the ways that count, isn't she?

I'm just glad she's okay. I don't know what I would have done if something had happened to her. I don't even want to go there.

Our apartment is kind of a mess now, though. Jen and I have taken to eating al fresco. At least that's what Jen calls it. To me, it's just eating out on the fire escape. But that's so Jen. She's able to see the beauty and adventure in even the littlest things. Although I have to admit that being in a fire was probably a little too adventuresome, even for her.

But Jen's right. There is something kind of romantic about being out there on the fire escape, all cuddled up under the stars, having a picnic dinner. Surprisingly, Jen did make something for dinner last night. She made the one thing she does really well: phone calls. That's right, we called in for pizza.

I think Jen felt kind of bad about my chair and my clock being ruined. I could tell, because my beautiful vegetarian wife let me get the pie half-pepperoni. But the truth is, the chair and the clock and anything else that may have gone up in smoke mean nothing to me. Sometimes it takes something really scary like this to make you realize that it's the people you love, not the things you've gotten used to, that really matter. Besides, maybe it is time that I got rid of all that old college junk. I'm past all that. Jen and I have started a new phase in our lives. It's time our apartment reflected that. We should put the place together, together. And we will. If we ever get enough money to buy anything.

Catch ya later.

—Jesse

Yours . . . Mine . . . Ours?

Jesse stumbled out of bed on Saturday morning and made his way over to the coffee machine. He blinked his eyes heavily as he entered the living room area. It had been several weeks since the fire, and almost a month since Jen had painted the walls of the apartment, but Jesse still couldn't get used to the color combination that his art-historian bride had picked out for the place. She'd painted the walls a deep burgundy color, and then painted the ceiling periwinkle blue. Jen had tried to explain to him about choosing opposite colors on color wheels, and how the warm walls seemed more inviting, and other artistic sorts of things, but Jesse wasn't 100 percent sure what she'd been talking about. He was just glad that Jen had taken it upon herself to do the actual painting.

But they still didn't have any furniture. Furniture took money, and with Jen still taking out student loans for college and using her jewelry sales to pay the electricity and gas bills, and Jesse's salary mostly going for the rent and food, there was no extra cash for furniture in the budget. They'd temporarily borrowed a card table and some folding chairs from Richie and Meg, so they didn't have to eat out in the fire escape anymore. All it had taken was one autumn windstorm for that experience to go from romantic to just plain insane.

As the coffee perked, Jesse went over to the computer to check his e-mail. He was sorry he'd ever given the people in his office his home e-addie. It seemed that every weekend someone from work was sending some assignment that was "just a little thing" they needed by Monday. Jen had been really sweet about giving him the space to work when he had to, but he missed spending lazy Saturday afternoons doing nothing with her. Still, on the other hand, Jen's grades had really gotten great since she'd had the extra time to study. Of course, that didn't seem to make either of them feel better about the lack of free time together.

Sure enough, as soon as he signed on, the computer set out a little beep, and an envelope icon began flashing on and off in the corner of the screen. For a moment, Jesse considered turning the machine off and pretending he'd never gotten any e-mail, but he eventually thought better of it. A junior employee couldn't mess around—especially with the way he and Jen depended on his salary and insurance plan.

The e-mails began piling up in his box. The first few were just unwanted spam—a couple of ads for cheap prescriptions for Viagra. Jesse had to laugh. They definitely didn't need that. Then, there was an e-mail from Jen's mother, who had finally gotten onto the Internet and was now absolutely obsessed with the idea of talking to her daughter and son-in-law online. There was an e-mail from someone in the marketing department at work, and another from Duets.

Jesse decided to open the Duets message first. He clicked on it and watched as the e-mail appeared on the screen. A moment later, he let out an excited shriek. "JEN! COME HERE! YOU GOTTA READ THIS!"

It would have been impossible for Jen to not wake up to that ear-shattering cry. She came racing out of the bedroom, not even bothering to throw on a robe.

Jesse stared at his wife in all her naked glory, and immediately leaped up to pull the shades. "What are you doing? Trying to give the whole neighborhood a thrill?" he asked her.

Jen laughed, but made no attempt to cover up. Instead, she asked, "What's the big deal? You woke me up out of a sound sleep."

Jesse pointed to the screen. "You're not going to believe this," he told her.

Jen nudged Jesse out of the way to get a closer look. Her eyes grew wide as she read the message from Duets.

Jennifer and Jesse,
We were sorry to hear about the fire in your apartment. So were a large number of our members and sponsors. In fact, one sponsor, Le Chien Furnishings, felt so bad, they are giving you a spectacular gift: a complete home makeover, including a table and chairs, book-

shelves, a computer desk and entertainment center, and a bedroom set. All you have to do is head over to one of their locations near you, pick out what you want, and give the attached coupon to the person at the register.

We're sure our members (not to mention the folks at Le Chien) would love to see what you've done with the apartment. When your home is all decorated, we'd adore it if you'd post a few pics on our site.

Happy shopping,
your pals at Duets

"Woohoo!" Jen grabbed Jesse and hugged him tight. "Do you believe this luck?"

Jesse shook his head. "What—the fact that Duets scored free furniture for us, or the fact that I am standing here holding an incredibly gorgeous naked brunette in my arms?"

Jen kissed him playfully on the nose. "Either-or," she teased. Then she looked into his eyes. "Can we go shopping today?" she pleaded, sounding very much like a little girl begging to go to a toy store.

"I have to do a little work for the marketing

department. Maybe you should go ahead and pick out at least some of the furniture on your own."

Jen shook her head. "No way, Jesse. This is *our* apartment now, remember. Not yours, or mine . . . *ours*. And we don't always have the same taste. You kinda freaked out when you saw the paint on the walls, remember? "

"I like it now," he told her. "Sort of."

"See what I mean?" she continued. "That's why we're going to shop together. Now I'm just going to hop in the shower and then we can head over to Le Chien."

"But what about my job?"

Jen gave him an especially sexy smile. "Oh, *I* have a job for you," she teased, playfully yanking on the belt of his robe. "One you're uniquely qualified for. It involves scrubbing that part of my back I can never reach while I'm in the shower."

The Le Chein store was really a huge shopping warehouse. Pieces of furniture were set up throughout the cavernous building. Every few feet there was a table with a catalog on it and order forms. Customers were supposed to take an order form and fill in the catalog code numbers of the furniture they wanted. Then an employee would go into the back of the store and pull out the large flat boxes that were filled with the furniture parts. Le Chien furniture didn't come set up. It was prefab furniture, which meant that it had to be assembled at home. Or, for an additional fee, a "carpenter" from Le Chien would come over and put it together for you.

"What kind of wood is this?" Jesse asked, running his hand over a shelf on a white armoire.

"It says MDF," Jen said, reading a tag on the side of one of the doors. "It must be a French abbreviation for something." She turned and caught the attention of one of the store employees, who was easily recognizable because, like all Le Chien sales staff, he was wearing a red beret and an apron. "What kind of wood is MDF?" she asked.

"Well, it's not any one kind of wood, exactly."

Jesse looked at the salesperson oddly. "Excuse me?"

"MDF stands for medium-density fiberboard," he explained in a whisper that demonstrated he felt he was revealing some sort of corporate secret. "It's pieces of compressed wood pulp mixed with glue."

"So it's not actual wood?" Jen asked, barely masking the disappointment in her voice.

"How do you think we keep the prices so low?" the clerk replied brusqely.

Jen had no answer for that. She simply sighed and stared at the armoire. "I like this one for the bedroom," she said, her voice lacking the excitement she'd had when they'd entered the store. "It matches the platform bed we picked out."

Jesse went over to the catalog table to look up the code number for the armoire. "The bed's called *Chaussure*. Sounds kind of romantic, doesn't it?" he said, trying to cheer her.

Jen shook her head. "*Chaussure* means shoe. Why would they name a bed that?"

"I don't know," Jesse admitted. "I guess they never expected anyone to actually translate the words. They just wanted everything here to have a French-sounding name to remind you that everything in the store was made in France. Like the entertainment center you picked out. That was called *Jambon*."

"Which means ham," Jen remarked, with just

a slight tone of amusement as she picked up a lamp that was sitting on a night stand and glanced at the bottom. "Hey. This was made in Taiwan, not France."

Jesse put his arm around Jen. He knew how much his wife adored really beautiful things. Not expensive things necessarily, just well crafted. Jen had an appreciation for design and craftsmanship that he would never completely understand. The stuff at Le Chien was made for mass consumption. There was nothing well crafted or intricately designed about it. This was useful furniture for people who didn't want to spend a lot of money.

Jesse sighed heavily. Someday he wanted to be able to buy Jen all the magnificent things she wanted. Unfortunately, today wasn't that day. Today, they would have to settle for French furniture that was made in Taiwan from wood that wasn't exactly wood.

"Well, that's about it," Jesse said, looking at the long list he and Jen had made up. "Unless you want that blue rug you saw."

"Periwinkle," Jen told him.

Jesse flipped through the catalog. "No. It says here it was called *Gâteu*."

"Cake," Jen translated the French ruefully. "No, I meant the *color* of the rug was periwinkle blue. Like our ceiling."

"Oh. Well, do you want it?"

"Might as well," Jen agreed. "We may never get the chance to get free furniture again."

"Okay, so let's go over to the check-out counter and give them our list. Then we'll go over to the loading zone. I think they'll help us tie all the boxes to the roof of the car." Jesse studied the big overhead signs until he spotted one that said, CHECK OUT. Jen followed him as he walked toward the cashier.

"Here you go," Jesse said as he handed the clerk his order form and the gift certificate from Le Chien that he'd downloaded from the computer e-mail.

"Would you like someone to come out to the house to put this together for you?" the clerk asked. "It's one hundred dollars extra, but it's not included in this gift certificate."

"That would be worth it, though," Jen mused. "These things look pretty tough to make."

"No, they don't," Jesse insisted. "I could do it in an afternoon."

"But Jesse . . . ," Jen began.

"Jen, have a little faith in the man you married. I'm pretty good with my hands . . . or haven't you noticed?"

Jen grinned. "I've noticed. But this is different."

"I can do it," Jesse told her firmly. He pulled out his cell phone. "I'll even call Artie to help so we can get this done twice as fast."

"Oh great, a businessman and a guy who's studying to be a divorce lawyer working together to put together furniture. Sounds promising," Jen teased.

Jesse shook his head. "O ye of little faith. Now, let's get the car and pull it around to the loading dock."

Jen nodded. But as Jesse swaggered off, she grabbed one of the Le Chien carpenter cards and tucked it in her pocket.

"How am I supposed to figure out anything from these stupid drawings?" Jesse barked angrily from the floor of the living room. He was literally buried in piles of MDF wood, nuts, bolts, and tiny screwdrivers. The instructions for putting the *Jambon* entertainment center together were spread out in front of him. "Would you look at this thing?"

Jen glanced down at the paper. Jesse was right. It would be impossible for anyone to follow the little stick-figure carpenters that were drawn on the pages of the instruction booklet. They were happy and smiling as they held up pictures of which screws were necessary to attach the shelving in the unit.

But Jesse certainly wasn't happy and smiling. In fact, he was downright snarky. Artie was even worse. He wasn't even attempting to put the furniture together anymore. Instead, he was sitting in the corner of the room with his head in his hands. "When I tie the nuptial knot, I'm going to buy custom-made furniture," he declared. "It's going to be delivered in one piece."

"Then you'd better tie that knot with an heiress," Jen suggested. "You wouldn't believe what furniture costs."

"I won't need to. I'm going to be wealthy on my own. There's always business for divorce lawyers. It's kind of like being a mortician. It's a business that everyone needs sooner or later."

"God, I hope not," Jen said, surprised.

"Not us, hon," Jesse assured her. He turned to Artie. "Will you hand me that screwdriver?"

"Which one?"

"The one with the little X in the top of it."

Artie looked in the small tool kit that had come with the furniture. "There are three of them that have X's on the top."

Before Jesse could respond, Artie's cell phone began to ring. He pulled the phone from his pocket, flipped open the top and looked at the number. "Hey, Babe," he said into the receiver.

Jen met Jesse's eyes. *"Babe?"* She mouthed to him, surprised.

Jesse shrugged. The concept that Artie knew anyone well enough to call them "babe" was news to him, too.

Artie walked into the bedroom and shut the door, obviously to have a little privacy.

"What was that all about?" Jen asked Jesse.

"Beats me."

"Maybe he was talking to a pig. You know, like the Babe in the movies." Jen giggled.

Jesse shrugged. "He said there was some assistant at the registrar's office of the law school who had been checking him out, but you know Artie. I figured it was all in his head."

"Well, that didn't sound like it was all in his head," Jen suggested. "Hey, *babe*," she repeated, imitating Artie's obvious attempt to be sexy when he answered the phone. The way Jen said it, she sounded like some skeevy guy in a bar.

Jesse began to laugh. Jen had Artie's act down perfectly.

"Well, you guys, I'm sorry, but I've got to say *adieu*," Artie announced, interrupting their laughter as he walked out of the bedroom.

Jen rolled her eyes. Artie had gone from overblown SAT words to French now. The furniture names must have been rubbing off on him. His ability to be pretentious seemed never ending.

"Felicia wants to take in a movie," Artie continued.

"*Felicia*, huh?" Jesse said. "Who's she?"

"Just someone who happens to think I'm a combination of Adonis and Einstein," Artie replied.

"Oh, Felicia's your mirror," Jesse teased his best bud.

"Amusing," Artie replied sarcastically. "But I've no time to guffaw. I'm off. Enjoy your construction work."

As Artie threw on his coat and walked out of the apartment, Jesse let out a frustrated groan. "Great. Now what am I supposed to do?"

"What? Artie was being such a help?" Jen asked him.

Jesse looked at the stick figures in the instruction book again. "This says a twelve-year-old could put this together," he read gruffly.

"Maybe I should go to the middle school down the block and get one to help you," Jen said, trying a little humor to bring him out of the funk he was in.

But Jesse didn't see the humor in anything at the moment. He was angry and frustrated. "Look, Jen, you're the one who wanted this entertainment center. I—"

"Oh no, you don't," Jen warned. "Don't pin this on me. We picked everything out together. We both wanted this piece—and the table, the bookshelves, the armoire, and the platform bed. The only thing I picked out myself was the rug. And, as you can see, I've already got that set up." She pointed toward the window, where the blue area rug had already been unrolled.

"Errrr!" Jesse let out a purely primal yelp of

anger as he tried banging two pieces of wood together in a fruitless effort to at least get the damn entertainment center started.

"I don't think that's quite right," Jen said gently.

The look in Jesse's eyes was positively rabid. He held the instruction booklet up. "You want to take a try?" he demanded.

"No. I can't do stuff like this," she told him. "I know my limitations."

"Are you saying *I* don't?"

"All I'm saying is that maybe home improvement isn't one of your talents. You're great at other things. You're smart, you're wonderful with numbers, you're funny, and you make people want to be around you. You just aren't terrific at putting things together. Big deal."

Jesse sighed. "Well, this is just great." He looked at the pile of pressed-wood shelving around him. "What are we supposed to do now?"

Jen took a deep breath. She was unsure of how Jesse would take what she was about to say. "Well, I did sort of take the carpentry card they had at the store. Maybe we could call and set up an appointment. It says someone could come by within forty-eight hours."

Jesse stared at her. The color rose to his cheeks. "You took the card?" he demanded. "You didn't believe that I could do this?"

Jen gulped. "Well, I . . . I mean, I wasn't sure. So, just in case I . . ."

"Thank God!" Jesse exclaimed, his face taking on a huge grin. "I'm glad one of us knew what was going to happen." He took the card from her hand. "Give me that number. The sooner we make this call, the sooner we can sleep on a real bed."

Men can be so impossible sometimes. What is this macho thing about wanting to do things that require tools? I've never seen that side of Jesse before. Not that I was surprised. My dad, who's the nicest guy in the world, also turns into a raving lunatic whenever he's faced with a challenge of hanging curtains or plastering a hole in the wall. Of course, he's terrible at it. One time Dad decided to lay the blacktop on our driveway, and wound up covering the surrounding grass, sidewalk, and bushes with that gooey stuff. My mom had to hire professionals to redo the whole thing.

I guess it's true what they say: Girls do marry people just like their dads.

Luckily, we're all set up now. The carpenter came this afternoon. It took him less than two hours to put everything in place. Even though Jesse was cool about having the work done, I'm glad he wasn't here to witness that!

You can see the pictures of our freshly decorated space by opening the attachment to this e-mail. But as for me, it's late, and I'm going to bed. Jesse and I are dying to break in our new bed. I sure hope MDF is strong enough to withstand all our wildness! ;)

Catch ya later!

—Jen

The Night the Lights Went Out

"We still need a five-letter word for 'browbeater,'" Jen mused as she stared at the Sunday crossword puzzle.

"How about 'bully'?" Jesse asked as he leaned over her and checked out their progress on the puzzle.

"You're a genius! Bully fits perfectly." She wrote the letters in the boxes and then stretched up her neck to kiss Jesse on the nose. "I knew that college degree of yours would come in handy someday. We've filled in nearly half the boxes."

"That's better than last Sunday," Jesse agreed as he sat down beside her and handed her a mug of hot cider. "Here you go, m'lady. I've even added a stick of cinnamon."

"Mmm . . ." Jen sighed contentedly as she curled up and buried herself in his chest. "You're spoiling me."

"Can't help it," Jesse told her. "You bring out the generous side of me."

Jen grinned. She loved these lazy Sundays. She and Jesse hung out until mid afternoon cuddled together, just the two of them with no contact with the outside world. They put on a CD—usually something quiet and classical (Jen's choice) like Brahms or Bach—and hung out.

"I think seven down is 'curmudgeon,'" Jesse said, staring at the puzzle. He grabbed the *Times Magazine* from Jen's hands and scribbled the word in the boxes.

"Sounds like my Nietzsche class professor," Jen moaned. "Talk about a cranky dude. You should see the paper he assigned us." She stood up from the couch and headed over to the computer table, where her backpack was sitting. "I don't even understand what he wrote on the syllabus, never mind what the assignment actually is."

"Whoa, get back here," Jesse ordered her. "Sunday is a no-work zone, remember?"

Jen stopped in her tracks, turned, and headed right back to the couch. She knew exactly what he meant. It was a decision they'd made before they'd even gotten married. Sunday was the one day a week they would just relax and enjoy each other's company. No exception. Lazy Sundays were sacred. "Sorry," she apologized as she snuggled back into his arms. "I'm just so obsessed with finishing off this semester."

"Just one more semester to go after that," Jesse assured her.

"*If* I pass this class," Jen moaned. "I just—" The sound of the downstairs buzzer interrupted her. She looked up, surprised. "Were you expecting someone?"

"Not me," Jesse said. "Maybe it's Artie stopping by or something."

"I hope not," Jen told him. "It's Sunday. *Our* day." Still, she leaped up and began straightening things up, beginning with the mountain of dirty dishes in the sink.

"Why are you putting dirty dishes in the broom closet?" Jesse asked her.

"You don't want whoever's at the door to think we're pigs, do you?" Jen asked. "Besides, I'll take them out and wash them as soon as whoever it is leaves." It was clear from her expression that whoever was at the door wasn't going to be around long.

Jesse shook his head and laughed. Jen was definitely one of a kind.

And so was Careen. Unfortunately, she wasn't Jesse's kind of person—which became abundantly clear when he opened the door. "What are you doing here?" he asked her pointedly.

Careen smiled. "Hello to you, too, buddy," she told Jesse as she walked right past him. In her arms she was lugging what appeared to be a huge canvas—maybe three feet tall—sheathed in silver and white wrapping paper.

"Why don't you come in?" Jesse asked sarcastically, knowing full well she'd already arrived . . . *uninvited*.

"J-squared, I know Sunday is private time—" Careen began.

"Don't be silly," Jen interrupted her. "We want our friends to always feel comfortable in our home." She smiled at Careen and Jesse. "Now I want you two to declare a cease-fire. Let's have a friendly visit, okay?"

Careen and Jesse looked at each other and

then nodded in unison. There was nothing either of them wouldn't do for Jen.

"I come bearing gifts," Careen said, handing the canvas in her arms to Jen.

"Ooh, presents," Jen squealed.

"Actually, just *present*," Careen corrected her. "Your wedding present."

"We got married almost three months ago," Jesse reminded her.

"Well, I've been working on it. You can't rush these things. Besides, I used it for my midterm critique."

"You're giving us a school project as a wedding present?" Jesse asked. He did not sound impressed by the idea.

Careen shook her head vehemently. "You've got that backward, Numbers Man. This *started out* as your present. It's just that it turned out so great, I had to used it for my critique." She turned to Jen. "Professor Haskell went nuts over it. He said if I keep going in this direction, I might be able to get a show in that new gallery that's opening in Jersey City."

"Careen, that's so exciting." Jen tore at the wrapping paper like a kid at Christmas, quickly revealing the artwork beneath. "Oh my goodness," she said with genuine admiration. "This is incredible. I've never seen anything like it."

"Me either," Jesse agreed, although his voice didn't share Jen's enthusiasm. "What is it?"

"I call it *J-squared*," she told him. "It's you guys."

Jesse stared at the painting. It was definitely a man and a woman. But that was where any comparisons to Jen and himself could be made. The man's body was thin and elongated, like a reflection in a fun-house mirror. His face was painted a pale gray-green, and his eyes looked frightened. The woman in the painting appeared to be floating overhead in a long white gown. Her face was tinted an odd shade of blue. Pieces of random objects, like the metal center of a computer disk, scraps from wine bottle labels, a computer printout, matchbook covers, and a few grains of dyed pink sand were scattered around the figures of the people. "That's supposed to be us?"

"Well, it's not you exactly. It's *representative* of you." She frowned and looked sheepishly at Jen. "I knew he wouldn't like it. I should have just gotten you some of those dishes your mother-in-law made you register for at Bloomingdale's."

"Are you nuts?" Jen said. "This is the best gift we've ever gotten. It's our first piece of real art. Don't worry. I'm teaching Jesse all about it. Once he begins to understand modern art, he'll recognize you for the genius you are." She looked around the living room. "I have just the perfect place for it. Over there, between the windows!" Jen pointed to a large space of wall where a poster from inside the Beatles' *White Album* was currently hanging.

"Wait a minute. That's a vintage poster," Jesse informed her. "It's probably worth a fortune!"

"But it's a *poster*," Jen countered. "This is real art. Besides, there were millions of that poster made. There's only one *J-squared*."

Jesse stared at the piece of art. "Thank God." He sighed. Still, he knew there would be no arguing with Jen now. "Well, can I at least move my poster into the bedroom?"

"Of course," Jen told him. "You can do whatever you want with it. This is your apartment too." She turned to Careen. "I know exactly the way I want this framed."

Careen blushed. "I would have framed it for

you," she said quietly. "But it's such an odd-size canvas. It would have cost me too much to frame it. I'm just a poor college student, y'know?"

Jen shook her head. "This is a great gift. You didn't need to do one thing more. I'll get it framed."

"Uh, just how expensive is it to frame a canvas that's not a typical size?" Jesse interrupted. "Because we have a lot of bills this month and—"

Jen stopped him before he could embarrass Careen. "Don't worry about it," she assured him. "I'll make it work within our budget."

Jesse didn't say anything. He just stood there, studying the green-faced, long-legged skinny creature that supposedly represented him.

"See, he's getting to like it already," Jen assured Careen.

Careen grabbed her pocketbook. It was obvious from the expression on her face that she wasn't sure Jesse would ever understand her work. "I gotta go," she said quickly. "I'll leave you two alone to get to know the painting."

Jen hugged her best friend tight. "This is the

greatest gift we ever could have gotten," she told her. "Thank you sooooooo much."

"My pleasure," Careen replied. "Just promise me one thing."

"Anything. What?"

"Snap a picture of your mother-in-law's face when she sees it. I would love to paint a picture called, *Adele Having a Heart Attack.*"

The image of her oh-so-uptight mother-in-law checking out Careen's avant-garde painting made Jen began to laugh so hysterically, a loud snort emitted from her nose.

"Mmm. Very attractive," Careen chuckled. "Was that what first attracted you to her, Jesse?" She walked over to the door.

"Thanks again," Jen told her. "I love ya."

"Me too," Careen assured her. "BFFE." Then she turned to Jesse. "No need for you to thank me, Numbers Man. The priceless expression on your face is gratitude enough."

Jesse sighed. "Thanks, Careen," he said. "It's definitely unique."

"Just like me," Careen chuckled as she left the apartment, closing the door behind her.

Jesse couldn't seem to take his eyes from the

painting. "You're determined to keep this in the living room?"

Jen nodded. "Jesse, you have no idea how talented she is."

"No idea," he agreed as he stared at the blue-faced flying woman. "No idea at all."

The painting had been hanging in the living room for more than two weeks, and Jesse still hadn't gotten to used to it. There was something innately creepy about the oddly shaped bodies and strangely painted faces. He saw them even when he closed his eyes. Yet, every time Jesse suggested taking the painting down, Jen went nuts. She'd even gone so far to suggest that the Lladró statues on the shelf were far more frightening to her than anything Careen could ever paint.

At least the frame was nice. Jesse had to admit that. He had a feeling Jen had spent a fortune on it, but she wouldn't tell him exactly how much. All she would reveal was that she got a great deal on the frame because she'd paid cash, and the guy who owned the frame shop was a cousin of someone in one of her art history classes. Jesse figured he had to trust that she wouldn't spend more than they could actually afford. After all, she knew just how much was in their bank account.

"Do we have any more popcorn?" Jen called over to him from the kitchen section of the room.

"I think we finished it last night," Jesse replied without lifting his head from the computer screen.

"Damn," Jen sighed. "I hate studying without popcorn. We don't have any chips either." She opened the refrigerator door. "Carrots. *Ugh*. Who ever heard of studying with carrots?" She took them out of the bin, anyway. "You want some?"

Jesse shook his head. "Nah, I'm still full from all that mac and cheese." He stared at the computer screen. "I'm almost finished with this spreadsheet. Just a few more figures and . . ."

At that moment, the computer screen went dark. So did all the lights in the room.

"What the . . . !" Jesse shouted. He began smacking his computer wildly.

"Forget it," Jen said, flicking the light switch on and off. "The power's off."

Jesse put his head in his hands. "But I was almost finished."

"Didn't you save it?" Jen asked hopefully.

"Not the last three pages," Jesse admitted. "Oh, man. It's going to take me hours to do that again." He stopped for a minute and looked out the window. "Funny, ours is the only building without power. I wonder what happened."

Jen stood up and went to the cabinet to get a few candles. The room was quiet—other than the sound of television in the next apartment. They could hear it coming through the walls.

Jesse sat there for a minute, confused. "Hey, how come they have power next door and we don't?"

Jen sat down for a minute. She seemed unsure of how to answer. Finally she answered, "I didn't think they were serious."

"You didn't think *who* were serious?" Jesse asked her suspiciously.

"The electric company," Jen answered very quietly.

"Why?" Jesse asked, his voice getting louder by the second. "Serious about what?"

"Well, about three days ago, they called and said if we didn't pay the bill, they were going to shut off the power," Jen blurted out in one long breath. "But—"

"We paid that bill!" Jesse shouted. "I put the check in the envelope myself. It was in that pile of mail that you were going to . . ." He stopped for a minute, staring at her face. She was looking guilty.

"I didn't mail that one," she told him in a voice that was barely a whisper. "If I had, I couldn't have gotten the cash I needed out of the account."

Jesse flinched. He had a feeling he knew the answer, but he had to ask, anyway. "What did you need the cash for, Jen?"

"For the picture frame," Jen told him pleadingly. "I paid cash because it was so much cheaper."

Jesse sat back in his chair and took a deep breath. *Stay calm,* he told himself.

But there was no staying calm now. "You didn't pay the electric company so you could spend the money on a picture frame for that piece of crap Careen calls art?" he demanded in a voice so loud, it could be heard across the state.

"It isn't crap at all. It's brilliant!" Jen defended

Careen's painting. "Don't criticize what you don't understand."

"Oh, I understand more than you think!" Jesse shouted back. "I understand that you behaved like a selfish two-year-old. I understand that you took *my* hard-earned cash and spent it on a frame for a painting *I* hate. Now we have no electricity, and I've lost hours' worth of hard work on the computer. That's what I understand, *Jennifer*."

Jen gasped. He'd never called her Jennifer before—at least not in that tone. He sounded like her mother had when Jen was a little girl and was caught doing something naughty. She hated being addressed that way.

"*Your* hard-earned cash?" she asked angrily. She was really mad now. And that took some doing, since Jen rarely got mad. "Since when is it *your* money in that account?"

Jesse sighed. Okay, that *had* been a low blow. "I just meant that when you're going to spend that much money, we need to discuss it first."

"That's not what you meant at all," Jen spat back. "You're just pulling some power play because you're working full time and I'm not."

"You could work part time, you know," Jesse pointed out.

"I *am* working part time."

Jesse gave her a haughty laugh. "What? Making jewelry and selling it at flea markets? You have to be kidding. What do you bring in with that—maybe sixty, seventy bucks a week? And you only get that much if you decide to actually spend a Saturday selling them. It's impossible for me to budget for anything when you're so damn mercurial."

"I can't work *every* Saturday. I have to keep my grades up," Jen defended herself. "You knew I wasn't going to be able to work that much while I was still in school. We talked about it before we got married."

"You won't be able to work when you get out of school either," Jesse retorted.

"What's that supposed to mean?"

"Oh, nothing. I mean there are tons of ads for philosophical art historians in the paper, right? Last Sunday, the *New York Times* had a whole page of them," he replied sarcastically.

"Boy, the apple doesn't fall far, does it?" Jen told him.

"Meaning?"

"Meaning that you're definitely Adele's little boy. It's all about cash with you, isn't it, Jesse?"

"That's not true, and you know it," Jesse insisted. "And don't turn this around on me. You were the one who went behind my back and bought an overpriced frame with the money we were supposed to spend on the electricity. You were the one who screwed up, Jen, not me. It's just another flaky move on your part. The only thing is, *I'm* the one who lost a whole night's work because of it."

"You wouldn't have if you'd bothered to save your work every few minutes. If you had, it would still be on the computer when the power gets turned back on."

"Yeah, well, by that time, I won't need it anymore. It's due tomorrow afternoon. I'm going to have to go into the office extra early tomorrow to do all that work over again."

For a moment, they just sat there silently in the dark, both stewing in their own anger. Neither one of them wanted to give in. Finally, Jesse stood up and headed into the other room.

"Where are you going?" Jen demanded.

"To sleep. It's too dark in here to do anything else, anyway."

"You can't go to sleep. Not *now*," Jen told him.

"Give me one good reason not to."

"We're in the middle of the fight."

Jesse sighed. "Excuse me?"

"You can't go to sleep angry, Jesse. It's a really bad thing."

"Yeah, well, so's sneaking money out of the account. So's ruining all my work. So's accusing me of being like my mother." His face was contorted with frustration and anger. The candlelight cast a sort of weird orangey glow on him.

Jen began to laugh.

"What's so funny?" he demanded.

"You. You look like one of Careen's paintings." Jen pointed him toward his reflection in the window.

Jesse stared at the frightening image. He did look like something Careen might dream up. He didn't like looking at himself that way.

He didn't like fighting with Jen either.

"Look Jesse, I'm . . ."

"Jen, I'm really . . ."

They both began to apologize at once, laughing when they realized how in sync they were.

"You go first," Jen told him.

"I'm sorry I said that about my money," Jesse told her. "You know everything I have is yours."

"Even the Lladrós?" Jen teased.

Jesse grinned. "*Especially* those."

"And I'm sorry I didn't talk about the frame with you first. It was stupid of me to use the apartment money on that. We should always talk about the big stuff. I know that."

"We should always talk about everything," Jesse told her. He turned and headed toward the bedroom.

"Where are you going?"

"To bed."

"But I thought we weren't going to sleep angry."

"I'm not angry anymore," Jesse assured her. "And I didn't say anything about *sleep*."

Jen got the message. She raced across the room, landing in his arms. Jesse held her tight for a moment, and then pressed her against the wall, pinning her there with his body. He kissed her hard, his tongue reaching hungrily into her mouth as his hands slipped under her T-shirt. He expertly slid the shirt over her head, and then followed by doing the same with his own. He held her tight against him, skin against skin, their hearts beating in unison. Jesse led her to the bed, and they lay down on the mattress, rolling around wildly, tearing at each other's jeans in a mad fury to rid themselves of the rest of the clothing they had on.

Jesse had never felt this way before. At this very moment, the need to feel her beneath him—*joined together with him*—was overpowering. It wasn't a mere desire. It was a genuine need. Like air, or food. A matter of his very survival. Making love with her was the only way to make sure that everything between them was all right again. And that was the most important thing in the world—more important than lights or computer power or money. Jen was his greatest life source.

As he clutched her even closer to him, feeling the smoothness of her soft skin against his body, he knew that this was the person he was meant to be with. It had all been part of some grand scheme. It was no accident that they'd found each other. This had been planned since the beginning of time. Their two souls would always be as one.

Jen looked up at him, her eyes filled with wild anticipation. Jesse grinned back at her, knowing exactly how she felt. With one strong, passionate motion, he felt himself inside her, their bodies now as connected as their souls.

Wow. I didn't think I'd be using this laptop again so soon. We've been in the dark for the past three days. I sort of screwed up and spent the electricity money on something else. Okay, not sort of. I definitely screwed up. (Bet you're not surprised to discover that Jesse was extremely pissed off at that.)

Luckily, I was able to earn enough money selling my jewelry at the flea market on Saturday to pay the electric bill. I don't usually sell that many pairs of earrings, but some mother and her daughter bought eleven pairs to give away as favors at the girl's birthday party. They were really fond of the ones with little pink- and green-haired trolls on them. Woohoo! Boy was I glad to be able to earn that money. Jesse and I went right down to the offices of the electric company. They turned the power on that very afternoon. Which was great—although I did kind of like the candlelit dinners.

What I didn't like was the fight Jesse and I

had over money. I have always hated fighting—
ever since I was a little kid. I was always the
one on the playground who played U.N.
between the kids who were arguing with each
other. You know, the one who urged everyone
to make love, not war. I'm just not big on con-
frontation. It scares me because people lose
control and say stuff they don't want to. And
you can't ever take it back. Not really, anyway.
The words that are said in arguments just sort
of hang there in the air like a heavy fog that
never completely melts away.

There is one good thing about fighting,
though: Making up is a lot of fun. And Jesse
and I were able to make good use of all that
darkness.

Anyway, I gotta get to class. Catch y'all later.
—Jen

Meeting the Ex

"Woohoo, pass the vino!" Careen cheered as she raced into Jen and Jesse's apartment, threw her book bag on the floor, and collapsed onto the couch.

"I can't believe we finally finished midterms week," Jen declared, joining her on the couch and pulling the bottle of chardonnay from the bag. "Now *that's* something to celebrate!"

"Assuming we passed everything," Careen reminded her as she went to the cabinet and helped herself to two elegant crystal wineglasses, part of a set that were a wedding gift from Jen's aunt and uncle. "I'm still a little shaky about how I did on that Psych 501 exam." She sighed heavily. "Why should an artist have to learn about neuroses, anyway?"

"Maybe so you can understand why all you artists are so crazy," Jen teased as she used a corkscrew to open the bottle and began pouring the celebratory wine. Then she laughed at Careen's insulted expression. "Kidding!" she assured her. Then she added, "I think they make you take it so you can learn about the human psyche, and then use that knowledge to add another layer to the meaning behind your work."

Careen mulled that one over for a moment. "Leave it to you to be logical." She sighed heavily. "I think Jesse's rubbing off on you."

"And that's a bad thing?" Jen asked. She raised an eyebrow suggestively. "Actually, I *love* when Jesse rubs me. Especially my back. The man gives the most amazing massages."

Careen screwed up her face. "Don't get all porno on me." She took a big gulp of wine, kicked her shoes off, and leaned back to relax. "So, what time are we hitting The Tavern?"

"I didn't know we were."

"Yeah, right. We've been at UNJ for almost three and a half years now and we've always celebrated the end of midterms week at The

Tavern," Careen reminded her. "Why should this year be different?"

"Maybe because this year I'm married?" Jen suggested.

"So?"

"Well, maybe Jesse won't want to go out tonight."

"Again, so?"

Jen sighed. "I don't know. It doesn't feel right going out partying without Jesse."

"But you do want to party with everybody, don't you?" Careen asked.

Jen grinned. "You know I do."

"Oh, thank goodness," Careen replied with exaggerated relief. "The old Jen is still alive in there somewhere."

Jen stuck out her tongue in Careen's direction, then poured herself another glass of wine.

By the time Jesse arrived home, the girls had pretty much polished off the bottle. They'd ordered in a pizza and were busy plotting and planning a way to get Jesse to agree to hit The Tavern, work night or not.

"Hey, my hot hunk of a husband," Jen said, leaping up from the chair and greeting him with a long, wet, sloppy kiss.

"Someone's been partying," Jesse said, laughing. "Last midterm went okay, I take it?"

Jen nodded. "I think I really killed on that Philosophy essay!"

"Awesome," Jesse congratulated her. He took off his overcoat and hung it neatly on the hook beside the door. Then he removed his sport jacket and laid it neatly over one of the kitchen chairs. Finally, he rolled up his shirtsleeve and grabbed a slice of pizza from the table. "How'd you do, Careen?"

"The jury's still out," she admitted. "But at least this lousy week is over. I swear, exams are a total pain in the ass!"

Jesse went over to the cabinet and took out a plate to put his pizza on. (Which was more than the girls had managed to do—they just ate out of the box.) Then he sat down at the table to enjoy his slice.

"Oh, why'd you do that?" Jen asked.

"What?"

"Take off your coat. We're leaving any second."

Jesse seemed totally confused. "Leaving? Where are we going?"

"To The Tavern," Careen informed him. "End-of-midterms celebration."

"Oh, no," Jesse said. "Count me out. I've got a big meeting tomorrow."

"Killjoy," Careen taunted him.

Jen flopped down in her chair and pouted like disappointed toddler. "Well, I guess that's out," she moaned.

"You can go ahead," Jesse told her. "I'm the one who has to work tomorrow."

"No. I can't have a good time if I know you're here slaving away," Jen told him. She sighed. "It was much more fun when we were both in school. At least then we were both on the same wavelength."

"You two were never on the same wavelength," Careen noted. "You were just on the same schedule."

Jesse didn't reply. Instead, he reached down and rubbed Jen's shoulders. "Go ahead. Seriously. You deserve it. Don't worry about me. I'll just look over my notes, crank up some music, and crash out."

"You sure?" Jen asked dubiously.

"Would I lie to you?"

Jen shrugged. "Well, since you put it that way . . . " She turned to Careen. "Just give me a few minutes to put on my makeup." Some of the earlier excitement was missing from her voice. It just wasn't going to be the same without Jesse.

"Hurry up," Careen urged. "Everyone's probably there already."

"Who's everybody?" Jesse asked matter-of-factly as Jen went into the bathroom to find her blush and lip gloss.

"Oh, our whole crowd. You know, Hilary, Brianna, Nathan, Alex, Alyssa, Dave, Julianna …"

"*Dave's* going to be there?" Jesse stopped her, his voice scaling up slightly.

"Sure," Careen said. "He's always there."

"*Jen's* Dave?"

"Well, he's not her Dave anymore," Careen reminded him. She pointed to the ring on Jesse's left hand. "Remember?"

"You know what I mean."

"Dave Morrison, Jen's ex, will be there," Careen told him. "But I wouldn't worry about it. He probably won't even know she's there. He's bringing his guitar. He'll be too busy serenading the single women to bother with Jen."

"He's bringing his guitar to a bar?"

"Why not?" Careen shrugged. "He brings his guitar anywhere. He plays whenever the muse strikes him. Jen must have told you about that. Heaven knows he wrote enough songs about her back in the day."

Jesse finished off his slice of pizza without saying a word. Then he put the empty plate in the sink, walked over to the coat hook, and slipped his winter coat back on.

"Where are you going?" Jen asked him as she walked out of the bathroom ready to leave. She shook her long brown hair a few times to fluff it up.

"With you," Jesse said, his eyes clearly registering how incredibly beautiful Jen looked in her low-slung jeans and tight blue sweater that matched her eyes perfectly. "I decided I wanted to help you celebrate. What am I, fifty years old or something? I'm a young guy. I can still go out for a few hours and go to work in the morning. I'll just take it easy so I don't have a hangover."

"Wow!" Jen exclaimed as she and Careen followed Jesse out the door. "What changed his mind?"

"Can't imagine," Careen replied.

Jen eyed her best friend knowingly. "What did you say to him?"

Careen laughed. "I just told him who was going to be there. I guess he just wanted to hang out with your old gang. Or at least be there when you did."

Jen watched as her husband bounded down the stairs of their apartment building. "You know," she said to Careen, "I think you probably did better than you think on that final. You really do understand psychology."

"No, girl. I just understand men."

The Tavern was really hopping by the time Careen, Jen, and Jesse arrived. It was as if the entire student body of the University of New Jersey had converged on the tiny neighborhood bar. Everyone was in a good mood—which could be explained by the smell of draft beer that hit them the minute they reached the door.

"Man, these floors are sticky," Jesse complained as they made their way over to the huge table in the back of the bar where Jen and her friends usually hung out. "It's going to ruin my new Kenneth Coles."

"What did you say?" Jen asked him, struggling to hear over the raucous sound of celebrating college kids.

"Never mind," Jesse shouted loudly into her ear. "You want a glass of wine?"

Jen shook her mane of long brown hair. "I'll just split the pitcher with everyone else."

"Well, I'm going to get a bottle of water. Save me a seat."

Jen nodded. "See you in a minute."

That was an impossible request. Jen's friends were crowded tightly around the series of small tables that they'd pushed together to form one long banquet-style table. There wasn't a chair to be found. Careen had managed to find a seat though—right on Louis's lap. At the moment, she was taking a hit off his cigarette. Louis was playfully running his fingers through Careen's long hair, which she'd just dyed a funky candy apple red.

Jen laughed. Careen changed her hair color more often than most people changed their sheets.

"Hey, Jen," a tall, lanky guy with long curly brown hair and deep piercing hazel eyes greeted her. His voice was lazy and relaxed, as though he'd be comfortable anywhere.

"Dave, hey," Jen replied in a matter-of-fact voice that could only mean that she'd long since gotten over him.

"Finish your midterms today?"

"I'm a free woman," she nodded, grabbing a glass from the table and pouring herself a beer from a nearby pitcher.

Dave looked pointedly at the thin gold band on her hand as she poured. "Not exactly—which is unfortunate for me and all the other men you've left behind."

Jen blushed. "I didn't exactly leave you behind," she reminded him. "Actually, I think it was *you* who said you couldn't handle monogamy. As I recall, you felt it wasn't a natural state of being for humans."

Dave laughed. "Sounds like me. So, where's your other half?"

"He's at the bar getting himself a drink."

"What? Our beer's not good enough for him?" Dave teased.

Jen shook her head. "No. He's got a big business meeting tomorrow."

"Business," Dave repeated in a quiet, scornful voice. "B.J. and the businessman. Who'd have thought it?" He took a sip of his beer and looked over toward the bar.

Jen followed his glance. It was obvious Dave was staring at Jesse. He was hard to miss. Even Jen noticed how out of place he seemed in the The Tavern. He hadn't taken the time to change before they'd left for the bar. So now, among a sea of blue-jeaned college kids, there he was in his dark gray wool slacks, blue and white pin-striped shirt, and red tie. His stylish, expensive haircut seemed strange among the other guys in the Tavern, most of whom had their hair in extremes—either long like Dave's, or cut so short, their scalps peeked through. At the moment Jesse was glancing down at his wrist, checking the time on his watch. No one else in the bar was even wearing a watch, never mind caring what time it was. They didn't have to. They had nowhere to be now that their midterms were finished.

Dave began to sing one of his old songs into Jen's ear. "With her kind, gentle eyes, and her long brown hair, she's my lady fair. A shimmering light who shares my dreams, my bed, my life . . ."

"That was a long time ago, Dave," Jen said, moving away so she could no longer feel his hot, beer-scented breath or hear his voice sounding so intimate.

"Not *so* long ago."

"How many women have you sung that one to since we broke up?" she demanded.

But Dave didn't seem at all confrontational. Rather, he seemed sort of sad. "No one. Never. That one's all yours, Jen," he swore, staring into her eyes in a way that made her incredibly uncomfortable. She moved closer to the wall, trying to increase the distance between them.

"Hey, honey," Jesse greeted Jen loudly as he suddenly sidled up to her, wrapping a strong muscular arm around her shoulder. He pulled her close and gave her a peck on the cheek. It wasn't a random act of affection, rather, it was a clearly calculated act that was designed to let Dave know Jen was out-of-bounds.

"Well, if it isn't *the husband*," Dave greeted him in a voice that was tinged with irony and condescension. "How's the rat race treating you? Tired of running in the maze yet?"

"Rats run in all sorts of circles, Dave," Jesse informed him in an equally condescending tone.

"So, uh, did you finish your midterms yet?" Jen asked Dave hurriedly. She made sure her body was physically between the two of them, hoping to stop any trouble before it started.

Dave shrugged. "Nah. I've still got one more tomorrow. Modern Poetry."

Jen took a sip of her beer. "I heard that was a good class. Louis loved the teacher."

"Professor Coleman's cool," Dave agreed. "But I don't always agree with her. Would you believe she thinks Dylan Thomas is *overrated*?"

"How could she say that?" Jen was incredulous.

"I don't know." Dave began quoting a poem by the Irish poet in a voice so melodic, it was hard not to get caught up in it. "'Do not go gentle into that good night,/Old age should burn and rave at close of day; . . .'"

"'Rage, rage against the dying of the light,'" Jen finished the stanza in unison with him.

Jesse looked at the two of them as though they were speaking another language.

"Magnificent." Dave sighed. "Brilliant imagery. Such anger. The prof's completely off her rocker."

Jesse finally couldn't take it anymore. He stared at Dave with disdain. "You've got a midterm tomorrow and you're here partying? What, are you nuts? Don't you want to get a decent grade?"

"Hey, you know. Live for today." Dave shrugged and took a big gulp of beer. "Besides, I figured I'd get a chance to see Jen." He turned and focused all his attention on her. "You don't hang out anymore. Your selfish husband here's keeping you all to himself." He looked over at Jesse. "That's not fair, dude. Everyone deserves a little B. J. from time to time."

Jesse's eyes glared. *B. J.?* "What did you just say?" he demanded.

"Relax, dude. It's not what you think. Get your mind out of the gutter." Dave laughed.

"It stands for 'Brown-haired Jennifer,'" Jen assured Jesse. She turned to Dave and smiled knowingly. "You know, as opposed to Tall Jennifer, Short Jennifer, Space Cadet Jennifer, Redheaded Jennifer . . ."

Dave laughed. "She wasn't a real redhead, did you know that?"

Jen shook her head. "No. And I don't really want to hear how you found out." She turned to Jesse. "The point is, Dave knew a lot of Jennifers, so he gave us each a special nickname just to keep us straight."

"But the name never really did you justice," Dave told her. "You shouldn't be a Jennifer. It's too ordinary. You need a name as unique as you are."

"Oh, I think I'm going to be ill," Jesse muttered under his breath.

"Hey, I've got my guitar," Dave told Jen, pointedly ignoring Jesse. "You want to sing harmony with me? We could do one of the old songs—maybe something by the Dead. You remember 'It Must Have Been the Roses'?"

"I never sang that one with you," Jen told him. "The Grateful Dead are my parents' idea of music, not mine. Maybe it was Space Cadet Jennifer. I think she was the one who liked to compare you to a young Bob Weir. Not me."

Dave sighed and took Jen's hand. "You gotta let go of the past."

"You gotta let go of *my wife*," Jesse ordered him.

"Hey," Dave said, moving away. "Chill out, man. I was just talking to an old friend. That's all."

"Really, Jesse, relax," Jen told him. "We're just friends."

"Yeah, right. Friends." Jesse didn't sound so sure. He looked around the table. "Isn't it funny that this whole place is filled with your friends, and yet you managed to find a spot right next to *him*."

Dave looked from Jesse to Jen. "Okay, this is where I leave." He reached behind him, picked up the guitar he'd stashed in the corner, and walked over to where Jen's friends Brianna and Hilary were sitting. He immediately began serenading the girls with one of his tunes.

"That guy's a real piece of work," Jesse snapped. "I can't imagine what you could have seen in him."

Jen studied his face. "Wow, Jess, I've never seen this side of you."

"What side?" Jesse demanded.

"The jealous side." Jen laughed.

"Yeah, right. Like I'd ever be jealous of that loser. He's on a fast track to nowhere."

Jen took a sip of her beer. "It's okay to be jealous, Jesse. I don't think I could stand to see you near one of your exes. I'd have to kill her." She looked up at him and wrinkled her nose playfully.

But Jesse was clearly not in the mood to play. "I'm not jealous!" he shouted—far louder than he'd planned. Everyone in the bar seemed to have heard him—it was obvious by the stares he got from the people around him, and by the slight chuckle that came from Dave.

"That's it. I'm outta here," Jesse shouted. He grabbed his wool overcoat and stormed out.

"Jesse, wait." Jen picked up her sky blue parka and hurried out of the bar after him.

Jesse didn't wait. He just kept going. Jen struggled to keep up with him. But it was hard. He was so much taller than she was. An icy rain had begun to fall. It was unusual for this early in November. Jen hadn't been prepared for it. She was wearing heels, and the sidewalk was slippery. But she couldn't think about that now. She had to catch up to him. She had to let him know that he had nothing to worry about. Dave was her past. Jesse was her now. Her future. Her forever.

"Jesse, please . . ." She was running. Suddenly, her foot slipped on a patch of ice. She fell to the ground with a thud. "Ow!" she cried out, more in shock than in actual pain.

But all Jesse heard was her cry. Instantly he turned around and raced back to help her. "Oh God, Jen, are you okay?" he asked her as he kneeled down beside her on the cold sidewalk.

Jen nodded slowly. She tried to struggle to

her feet, but suddenly her ankle began to throb. "Oh man, I think I twisted it," she groaned.

"We gotta get you home," Jesse said. "Get some ice on your ankle."

Jen looked around ruefully at the slippery ground. "I think ice was the problem."

Jesse shook his head. "No. Actually *I* was the problem," he admitted. "I should have been better behaved in there. It's just that I . . ."

"You were jealous."

Jesse shook his head. "No. I was . . ."

"You were jealous," Jen repeated.

"Okay, so I was jealous," Jesse admitted in one forced breath. "I can't help it. I mean look at the guy, Jen."

"I've seen him."

"That's the point. You've seen him. And he's seen you. *All* of you."

"Oh God, is that what's bothering you? Don't be ridiculous. You knew you weren't marrying a virgin, didn't you? I mean come on. This is 2005! You weren't a virgin when we met, were you? And I'm glad about that. I've *definitely* benefited from your experience." She smiled, trying to tease him into loosening up a bit.

But Jesse wasn't in the mood for jokes. "It's not just that. It's everything. You guys share a whole past. All sorts of things. Dave understands a whole side of you I'll never get. That whole Bob Thomas poetry song lyric thing."

"That's Bob Dylan and Dylan Thomas," Jen laughed. "One's an old-time singer. The other's a poet. Well, actually a lot of people consider Bob Dylan a poet, too, but—"

"You see what I mean?" Jesse interrupted her.

Jen shook her head and sighed. "So Dave reads poetry. Big deal. He's also a class A jerkoff. He treats every woman he knows like shit."

"So why would you have . . ."

"He's a bad boy," Jen explained. "There's a certain attraction to that. At least at first. Dave's the kind of guy every girl should date once—just to get that whole bad-boy appeal out of her system."

Jesse looked at her, confused. She didn't seem to be making any sense.

"Jesse, don't you get it? If I hadn't dated Dave, I wouldn't have been able to fall in love with you. I wouldn't have been able to see what makes you right for me. I never would have appreciated how lucky I am that you're willing to spend your life with me."

"Lucky?" Jesse repeated. "*You? Jen, I'm* the lucky one. And if I ever lost you . . ."

"I'm not going anywhere," she assured him. "But you and I have Dave to thank for that."

Jesse looked at her with surprise. "*Thank Dave?*"

"Sure," she assured him. "Everyone I've ever dated—hell, *ever known*—was just a preparation for you. Just like every girl you ever were involved with made you ready for me."

She reached up and wrapped her arms around his neck. He looked down at her and kissed her passionately, pouring his relief into her with every movement of his lips.

Jen pulled away from him for a minute. "Uh, Jesse?"

"Yes?"

"It's kind of cold down here. My butt's freezing off."

"Oh, yeah. Wow," Jesse stammered. "Sorry. Here. Let me carry you. It's just a block till we're home." He lifted her up from the icy sidewalk and began to carry her down the street, taking care not to slip himself.

Jen leaned up against his chest and clung to him as he began trudging toward their building.

She was quiet for a moment, enjoying the feeling of safety and comfort in his arms.

Then another kind of feeling began to wash over her. Her whole body began to react to his nearness. "Jesse?" she said quietly.

"Yeah?"

"I really liked that kiss."

"Me too."

Jen was quiet for another moment. Then, again: "Jesse?"

"Yeah, hon?"

"Could you walk a little faster?"

"Sure." He looked at her with concern. "Are you okay? Do you need aspirin or something?"

"*Something,*" she agreed, in a quiet, breathless, excited voice. "But not an aspirin. What I need is *you.*"

Jesse grinned broadly and immediately picked up the pace. "Your wish is my command."

History. It's something I never was very good at. Not in school. And apparently not in life. I'm finding it really hard to accept that Jen has a history without me. I kind of like to think that our lives started when we met. It's a nice fan-

tasy.

But that's all it is: a fantasy. The truth is, there were guys who were important to Jen before I was. And I'm just going to have to accept that. The same way Jen says there were girls who were important to me before she was.

The thing is, before Jen I was too busy getting good grades and keeping my eye on the brass ring to take the time to fall in love. It didn't seem important. But once she walked into my life, I saw how wrong I was. Love is what's really important. And I do love Jen.

Which, I guess, is why I'm afraid of losing her to someone who is more like she is. Someone who appreciates the things she loves, like art and philosophy and poetry. Someone like that jerk, Dave.

That's why today I did something I never thought I would do. I went online and ordered two poetry anthologies. They're coming in the mail this week. And I'm going to read them cover to cover, think about them, and try to discuss them with Jen. I'm going to try and enter her world a little bit.

But fair's fair. If I'm going to start reading poetry or going to look at bizarre art in gal-

leries, then Jen's going to have to try some new things too. So, as long as I was online, I ordered us a pair of tickets for opening day at Yankee Stadium. Hey, she might even like base-ball. I've heard a lot of women say they appre-ciate watching Derek Jeter run around the bases. . . .

Which just means I'll have to try to not get jealous all over again (LOL!).
—Jesse

The Business of Business

Jen sat in front of the computer and stared at the screen. She hadn't written for the Duets Web site in a while. But since Sonja, the head of their "Special Projects" department had just sent her an early-morning, no-so-gentle reminder of her deal to chronicle the first year of her marriage, Jen figured she'd better get on it. Especially since Jesse hadn't gotten a similar note from Duets. Naturally, *he* was all caught up on his quota of e-mails. Jesse was great at things that required a sense of responsibility. Jen, not so much. But she was working at it. Like right now.

Let's see. This week I got back most of my midterms, and I'm running about a 3.7 this semester. That's pretty good. Keeps me on the honor roll, and that means I can continue getting my partial scholarship, anyway. My cume would have been even higher except for this hard-ass Philosophy prof I've got. You've never seen anyone so petty about grading essays.

Anyway, in between classes, I've been making lots of jewelry—my new thing is wire snakes. I'm braiding copper or aluminum wire into thick ropes, and then making them into snake-shaped bracelets, ankle bracelets, and rings. They're pretty cool—especially when I use little red stones to make the eyes.

Tonight's going to be pretty nerve-racking. We're supposed to go out with three other couples. I don't know any of them. Jesse works with the three husbands. Which means I'm going to be one of the wives. Up until now, I've loved it when Jesse has called me his wife. The word made me feel all warm and safe inside. But the way he said it the other night when he was talking to one of his coworkers, "I'll have to run that by the wife," really freaked me out. The wife. What's that about? He might as well have called me the little woman.

But that's what I'm going to be tonight. The wife. And the youngest wife at that. Jesse's the new guy in his department. Most of the people there are in their thirties. These wives haven't been in school in a long time. From what I gather, they're real soccer moms—spending their days shuttling their kids from dance class to soccer practice, to the mall and back again. At least that's what they do when they're not taking Pilates classes or getting manicures.

What the hell am I going to talk to these people about?!

At least we'll eat well. Jesse said the head of his unit was going to put it on his business expense account. We're going to this little Italian place. Jesse says it's pretty fancy, so I've got to get going and pick out an outfit.

Peace out!
—Jen

Jen smiled with self-satisfaction as she pressed the send icon and walked away from the computer. Another task crossed off her list. That is, if she actually kept a list. Jesse was always bugging her to make a list of the things she had to get done on a daily basis. That way she wouldn't be so forgetful. But Jen was pretty sure she'd lose the list if she made one, so what would be the point?

She opened the closet door and stared at her wardrobe. She needed something festive and a little fancy for the evening. But that was easier said than done. Mostly, Jen's wardrobe consisted of jeans, T-shirts, and sweaters. She did have a few skirts—a couple of pleated miniskirts (which would be too Britney in her "Hit Me Baby One More Time" phase for tonight), and a couple of flowing Indian gauze kind of things (they had a slight hippie feel to them, which thrilled her mother, who hadn't changed her own wardrobe since 1973). Not much to choose from.

Finally she settled on a pair of tight, low-cut black pants with shiny silver zippers on the calves and pockets. She paired them with a clingy, shimmery, silver shirt with a low scoop neck and three-quarter sleeves.

"Hmmm . . . not bad for *The Wife*," she mused as she studied her reflection in the mirror. Then she hung her head upside down, shook out her brown hair, and flipped it back as she stood up straight. Just the look she was going for: hot housewife.

Now there was nothing left to do but wait. She went into the living room, sunk down into the couch, and picked up her Nietzsche text. Jen was determined to pick that grade up—despite the professor.

But she'd barely had time to begin the chapter when Jesse appeared at the door. "Honey, I'm home," he shouted out, sounding very much like the husband on that old fifties *Leave It to Beaver* sitcom.

Jen leaped up off the couch and greeted him with a very un-fifties kiss. (It was more like new-millennium *Sex and the City*, considering the incredibly limber things Jen could do with her tongue!) When she finally released him from her grasp, she stepped back and spun around like a model on a runway. "You like?" she asked.

Jesse didn't answer right away.

"You *don't* like?"

"No, you look great," Jesse assured her. "It's just that . . . well . . . It's a little clingy, don't you think?"

"It's too clingy? Why? Do I look fat?"

Jesse laughed. "You? Are you nuts? You look hot as hell. Which is sort of the problem."

"Looking hot is a problem?"

"It is when you're out with *these* people. They're kind of conservative."

"Oh," Jen tried to hide her disappointment. "Well, give me a minute. I'll try something else."

She headed into the bedroom, only to emerge a few minutes later in one of her long skirts—an emerald green gauze, with a blue and green blouse. She'd added long silver chandelier earrings to the ensemble.

"How's this?" she asked, twirling around so the skirt opened wide around her. "Ooh, that's fun," she squealed, turning again.

Jesse frowned. "Well . . ."

Jen eyed him cautiously. "Well what?"

"It's kind of like a gypsy thing, isn't it?"

"Excuse me?"

"I just feel like all you need is a tambourine and you could be that Esmeralda character in *The Hunchback of Notre Dame*."

Jen's eyes opened wide. "Well, if it isn't Mr. Blackwell," she snapped at him. "Who else is on your worst-dressed list tonight?"

"Come on, Jen, that's not fair," Jesse replied. "You know I think you're gorgeous in anything. But these are the people I work with. And they're different from, well, say, than Careen."

"Bummer for them," Jen spat back. "What are they, more like Artie?"

"Hey, don't put Artie down," Jesse told her. "He spent his lunch hour helping me pick these out for you." He reached into his jacket pocket and pulled out a small blue velvet box.

"Oooh, a present!" Jen's tone changed immediately. "Hand it over."

Jesse couldn't help but laugh at her childlike excitement. "I hope you like them."

"I'm sure I will," Jen assured him, grabbing the box from his hand. "You have incredible taste." She opened the box. *At least usually,* she thought as she stared at what was inside the book. *How awful.* She had to fight to keep a smile on her face. "Pearl earrings?"

Jesse nodded. "You like them? They're real cultured pearls. And those are real sapphire chips, too."

"They're, um . . . they're not like anything I have," Jen said slowly.

Jesse beamed. "I know. It's funny, the minute

Artie picked them out I realized why I like them so much. They're so classy. You know, my mother has a pair just like them—except the sapphires are a lot bigger."

"Your mother?" she nearly choked on the words.

"Yeah. Say what you want about her, my mother's got a good sense of what looks classy on a woman."

"Classy." Jen was having a hard time digesting all of this. It seemed all she could do was repeat bits and pieces of what Jesse was saying.

"Hey, you know what? You have a dress that would go perfect with those," Jesse noted excitedly.

"I do?" Jen didn't sound so sure.

"Yeah, I remember seeing it when we first moved in. Come on, I'll find it."

Jen followed him into the bedroom, still staring at the cultured pearl and sapphire-chip earrings in her hand. She really wanted to love them. But they just weren't her style. Still, it seemed so important to Jesse that she wear them. So she pulled the sterling chandeliers from her ears and replaced them with the pearls.

"Here it is!" Jesse announced as he reached way into the back of the closet and pulled out a plain black wool A-line dress with a high collar. "It's perfect."

Jen frowned. "Jesse, I bought that thing to go to my grandmother's funeral. I haven't worn it since."

"Oh," Jesse replied. "I didn't realize the dress had bad memories for you."

"It's not that. It's just that it's so . . ."

"Well, maybe you have something else in here that's kind of the same," Jesse continued. He began to slide the hangers, looking for a dress.

Jen sighed. "It's all right," she told him finally. "I'll put on the black dress. May as well get another wearing out of it, anyway."

"That's great!" Jesse exclaimed, stepping away from the closet. "You're going to look gorgeous. Every woman looks great in a little black dress."

Jen laughed despite herself. "Where'd you get that from?"

"Artie," Jesse told her.

"Oh, I didn't know he'd become a fashion expert. What, is he working for Versace now?"

Jesse shook his head. "Very funny. Actually, I think he said he read it in a magazine."

"Probably *Morticians Monthly*," Jen murmured to herself as she slipped the funeral dress over her head.

The party from the business office was easy to spot. Jen knew who they were as soon as she and Jesse entered the restaurant. They were seated at a round table on the far end of the restaurant. The men were dressed in dark sports jackets, shirts, and ties. The women were all dressed equally as uptight. One woman was wearing a dark purple sweater set over a pair of gray wool slacks. Another had on a chocolate brown blouse and a brown-and-cream-colored long skirt. The third woman was wearing a navy blue skirt with a cream-colored cashmere sweater. *Extremely conservative*. And they were all wearing pearls. Lots and lots of pearls. Jen sighed quietly and nervously fingered one of her pearl earrings.

"Hey, Merriman, over here." One of the men, a tall guy with dark hair that was garying at the temples, waved to Jesse.

"Why do men always call each other by their last names?" Jen whispered to him.

"'I don't know. It's just a guy thing," he replied.

"Well, what do I call him?" Jen asked.

"Steve. That's his name."

"Steve," Jen whispered to herself, putting the name and face together in her memory bank.

"And the short, chubby bald guy is Barry," Jesse told her. "He's the head of the unit. The other one's Charlie. You've talked to him on the phone before."

"Steve, Barry, and Charlie," Jen repeated as they crossed the room to join their party. "Gotcha. And who are the women?"

"I don't know. I've never met them."

"Don't they ever talk about their wives at work?"

"Not by name. They usually just say 'my wife.'"

Jen frowned. She wondered if she, too, was just one of the faceless, nameless, corporate wives.

Apparently not. As they reached the table, Barry stood up and pulled out a chair for her. "Ah, the mysterious Jennifer," he greeted her with a jolly smile. "Your pictures don't do you justice."

"My pictures?"

"Merriman here has a whole shrine to you in

his cubicle," Steve informed her. "We give him grief about it all the time."

"They're newlyweds," the woman in the cashmere sweater reminded him. "I remember when we were like them." She reached out a perfectly manicured hand with a huge pearl and ruby ring on one finger. "I'm Andrea."

"Jennifer."

"And this is Marla and Helene."

"Hi," Jennifer said. She was glad the women were wearing different outfits. Otherwise she might have had a tough time telling them apart. They all had the same style of hair: medium length, reddish-brown with blond highlights, and parted on the side—although Helene's was curly while Andrea and Marla had straight hair. All three women were extremely thin—it was obvious they had plenty of time to work out. And they all had the same tight smiles on their lips.

"Did you have any trouble finding the place?" Barry asked as Jesse took a seat.

"We just got a little lost at the turn," Jesse said. "But Jen was able to figure it out. She's got an amazing sense of direction."

"I don't let Marla near a map," Charlie laughed.

Jen took a deep breath. A whole night of condescending talk like this might very well kill her. She raised her hand slightly in the air. "Excuse me," she called to the waiter.

Instantly he was by her side. "Yes, miss?"

"Would it be okay to order a drink?"

"Of course. What would you like?"

"How about a cosmopolitan?"

"Oh, certainly," the waiter replied. "I'll have to see some identification first."

Jen nodded and reached into her bag to pull out her wallet.

"Boy, I'd kill to be carded again," Andrea laughed.

"Youth is wasted on the young," Helene mused.

"I guess I'll just have a Coke," Jesse said. "I'm our designated driver." He turned and gave Jen a glance. It was obvious he wasn't pleased with her drink selection. Jen ignored his glance.

"You know, as long we're ordering, I think I'll have a vodka and tonic," Barry announced.

"Oh no you don't," Helene warned him, patting his middle-aged bulging belly. "No alcohol on the South Beach Diet. Too many carbs."

Barry rolled his eyes, but told the waiter, "I'll just have a Pellegrino, please."

"I'll have a Pellegrino as well," Helene added. "I have to get up early to take Alexis to her skating lesson."

"Well, I'll have a martini," Steve said. "With two olives, please."

"I'll have a Scotch and soda," Charlie added his drink to the list. "It's going to rain tomorrow, so my golf game's going to be canceled, anyway. I can sleep in."

"That's what you think," Marla told him. "You've got to get up with me. If you're not playing golf, you can take Dougie to his karate class."

As the waiter walked off with the drink order, Jen sat back in her chair and tried to pay attention to the conversation at the table. But it was hard. The men had already broken off into a group of their own, discussing industry gossip, while the women were busy discussing the new spa they'd discovered in the next town.

"Adriana gives the most incredible facials," Helena was saying. "I tried the oxygen one. It got rid of so many of those tiny lines."

Andrea nodded. "Do they do Botox there?"

Helene shook her head. "Only facials and wraps. The seaweed wrap was amazing. It got rid of so much cellulite."

Jen looked out across the restaurant, hoping against hope that the waiter was coming with the drinks, or to take the food order, or even just to tell them that one of them had left their lights on in the car. Anything to get them off this boring topic.

And then a miracle occured! Not only did the drinks arrive, but the waiter asked to take their food order. Okay, so it wasn't a major miracle, but beggars couldn't be choosers, could they?

"I'll have a Caesar salad and . . ." She paused for a moment. "What's an alfredo sauce?"

"A cream sauce, very rich, very good," the waiter told her.

"Ooh, yummy. I'll try that," Jen said cheerfully. She was happy to be able to order a salad and a main course. Usually, their budget limited them to one or the other.

"I'll try the house salad and the meatballs and spaghetti," Jesse ordered.

Jen had to stifle a giggle. That was so Jesse. Order what you know. Be safe.

"Oh, meatballs and spaghetti. That sounds good." Barry sighed.

"But not for you," Helena reminded him. "No carbs."

Jen shot Jesse a look. He thought she was bad for ordering the drink. How would he like it if she were to do that to him? She took a sip of her drink and smiled at the thought of it.

"I guess I'll have the Caesar salad as well, but no croutons," Barry agreed. "And the salmon."

"I'll have the roasted chicken," Helena told the waiter.

As the others gave their orders, Jen continued sipping quietly on her drink. The cosmo was sweet and it went down so easily. It wasn't like those crappy ones they made at home with cheap vodka. A warm feeling began to take over her, and she ordered another one.

As the conversation started up again, Jen drifted off, looking around the restaurant. It was a cute place, decorated with frescoes and fountains that were supposed to be representative of Italy. The tables all had little red and white gingham tablecloths on them. The place was very festive—even if most of the clientele were pretty stuffy.

Within a few minutes the waiter arrived with their appetizers and a fresh cosmo. Jen took a sip and she waited until everyone had their food. (Hey, she hadn't been raised in a barn!) Then she dove into her Caesar salad with such gusto that everyone at the table had to look.

"You're a little hungry, huh, Jennifer?" Steve teased her.

Jen wiped her mouth and looked up from her food, a little embarrassed. "I didn't really get to eat much today. I had to study my Nietzsche textbook, and I had to make some earrings for a friend. So . . ."

"Oooh," Andrea squealed, suddenly interested in something Jennifer had to say. "You make jewelry? How exciting. Do you cast in gold or silver?"

"Actually, I—," Jen began.

"Jen's jewelry is more avant-garde," Jesse interrupted. "She uses various materials."

Jen shot him a look.

"Oh. Do you use crystals?" Marla asked. "I *love* Austrian crystals."

"Actually, I use a lot of copper wire. Some crystals. Lately I've been using subway glass."

The three women looked at her oddly.

"You know, when they redo a subway station, they have to break down the mosaic tiles and glass on the walls. Then they just throw it away. So my friend Careen and I go and take what we want. The tiles and glass are so interesting. You can do a lot with them. See?" Jen reached across the table and showed off one of her snake bracelets. It was made of copper wire and had small pieces of thick blue glass runing up and down the snake's body. The eyes were made of a green crystal.

Jesse's eyes bugged. He hadn't realized Jen still had the bracelet on.

Jen smiled triumphantly in his direction. He could try to make her over with the black dress and pearls, but she was going to remain herself no matter what.

"How interesting," Marla cooed. But she didn't really seem interested in Jen's jewelry making any longer.

Helene took a bite of her breaded-clam appetizer and smiled. "Mmm. This is amazing. I'm going to have to take three aerobics classes to make up for it."

"I'm into Pilates these days."

"Speaking of aerobics," Jen interrupted, the

cosmo suddenly giving her the courage to join the conversation, "did Jesse ever tell you guys about our honeymoon in Bermuda?"

The men stopped what they were saying and gave her their undivided attention.

"Uh, Jen," Jesse tried to stop her.

"No, not that, silly," Jen teased him. "A lady never kisses and tells."

Jesse sighed and leaned back in his chair. There was no stopping her now.

"I'm talking about the water aerobics classes in the pool," Jen assured her husband. "You know, the ones the German tourists took."

"I tried water aerobics a few times," Helene said. "But I hated getting in and out of the water. The chlorine wreaked havoc with my skin."

"Well, skin was all we saw at these classes," Jen giggled. "Jesse and I couldn't believe it. One minute, the German women were all sun-bathing topless. The next minute, they were in the pool taking water aerobics . . . also topless."

"Oh, no." Charlie laughed. "I wish I'd seen that."

Jen took another sip of her drink. "It was

positively surreal. All these half-naked women bouncing up and down doing jumping jacks and high kicks. And some of them had the hugest boobs. I swear, I don't know how they kept from whacking themselves in the face."

Jesse slid down deep into his chair and buried his head in his hands.

On the ride home, Jesse was very quiet. Jen, however, chattered on, the result of the three drinks (she'd had one "for dessert").

"The men you work with seem okay," she said. "A little dull, but you know, okay. Their wives, though. Boy. They couldn't talk about anything. Bo-ring!"

"I wish you'd followed their lead," Jesse muttered under his breath.

"What?"

"Nothing," Jesse said quietly.

"Yes it was. You said something. What was it?"

"Jen, you knew tonight was important to me. Did you have to act like that?"

"Like what?"

"You know, all giggly and flirty. Did you

have to tell that stupid story about Bermuda?"

Jen stared at him. "You like that story. You tell it all the time."

"Sure. To our friends. But these people . . ." He paused for a minute. "Couldn't you have just tried to fit in? Just for one night?"

Jen shook her head vehemently. "Why would I want to do that? Why would I ever want to spend even one minute talking like those women?" She pursed her lips tight and sat up very tall in her seat. "'I just love the seaweed wrap. Oh no. Not me. I like Botox.'" She rolled her eyes.

Jesse laughed in spite of himself. "I guess they were kind of dull," he admitted.

"Kind of? If I ever get like that, just take me out in the woods and shoot me!"

"Deal," Jesse told her. He smiled. "And if I ever start looking like Barry, promise me you won't pat my tummy in a restaurant?"

"Oh, you'll never start looking like Barry," Jen assured him. "Not if I can do anything about it."

"What are you, my personal trainer now?"

Jen nodded. "Oh yes. And as soon as we get home, I'm starting you on a very *personal* fitness program."

"Hmmm . . ." Jesse licked his lips. "Sounds good to me. Just do me one favor."

"What?"

"Keep the pearl earrings on."

"What is this, some new fetish—the house-wife and the businessman?"

"Could be fun," he told her suggestively.

Jen placed her hand on his thigh and laughed as the car swerved slightly. "Okay, the earrings stay," she agreed.

My wife is amazing.

I just want to put that in print. Actually, Jen made me write that, especially after she was such a hit with my boss. The guys I work with adored her. They thought she was interesting and fun. Steve even invited us to go fishing on his boat next summer. (Jen thought that was especially funny—maybe Andrea can get some fresh seaweed for her next wrap at the spa.)

I don't know why I ever doubted that Jen could wow over the guys from work. She didn't need to change her clothes, or talk about spas and golf. She just had to be Jen. I should have realized that the amazingness of her would be easy for anyone to recognize and fall in love with.

   After all, I did.

—Jesse

P.S. Okay Jen, I wrote it. Are you happy now?

A Turkey of a Thanksgiving

"Jen, can I braid your hair?" Samantha asked, crawling up on the couch beside her.

"That's *Aunt* Jennifer," Megan reminded her daughter.

"Oh, it's okay," Jen told her. "I don't mind being called Jen."

"You're family now," Megan said firmly. "She should call you by your proper title."

Jen shrugged. "Whatever you say, Megan."

Jesse reached over and put a protective arm around Jen. He knew this was hard for her. Thanksgiving with the Merrimans could be overwhelming—even to people who'd been born into the family. He could only imagine what Jen must be thinking.

He would have to imagine it, because Jen wasn't saying much. In fact, she'd been awfully quiet the whole way down to south Jersey, where Meg and Richie lived. She wasn't angry or anything. Just kind of dreamy and distant.

Jesse figured she was just nervous about having to spend the weekend at Meg and Richie's. He didn't exactly blame her. His sister-in-law, Meg, could be a bit much to handle. She was obsessed with perfection—the china, napkins and silver all had to be lined up perfectly. She'd made the turkey herself, a fact that she had made abundantly clear when asking Jen and Jesse to "just bring yourselves. We all know what happens when Jen cooks." Jesse had been ready to spit nails after that comment, but Jen had just laughed, volunteering to go to a local bakery and buy a cheesecake for dessert.

"Jen, you want a martini?" Richie asked. He was standing by the wooden bar in the family room. It was your typical suburban thing—it even had a round lamp on it that had the word "bar" written on the globe of the lamp, and a little drunken man leaning against it.

"No thanks," Jen said, wincing slightly as Samantha stuck her chocolate-covered hands into her hair and pulled hard, creating what Jen was sure was a tangled mess. "Are you positive you know how to braid hair?" she asked the girl.

"Sure," Samantha assured her. "I practice on my Barbie head all the time."

"Oh, my God, he's going for the touchdown!" Jesse's dad, Sam, cried out from his spot on the couch. "Richie, get over here!"

Immediately, Richie slammed down his martini shaker and ran over to the couch to get a glimpse of the game. He flopped onto the couch, forcing Jen to move to the edge—nearly throwing her to floor in his excitement. "Oops, sorry," Richie apologized without taking his eyes from the screen.

"These men and their football games." Adele sighed. She took a sip of her vodka Gimlet. "We women have much more interesting things to talk about."

"I'll say," Meg agreed. "Jen, why don't you come hang out in the kitchen with me and get away from all this nonsense?"

Jen didn't feel like being stuck in the kitchen with Perfect Meg, but she didn't see any way out of it. Dutifully, she got up from the couch and followed Meg into the kitchen.

"I've been up since six," Meg sighed as she opened the oven door and peeked in on the turkey. The smell of crisping skin and baking biscuits filled the room with warm, homey smells. It was extremely inviting, a sharp contrast to Meg's stark, oh-so-clean black-and-white kitchen. Usually, the kitchen was the most welcoming place in a house. But not at Perfect Meg's. Everything was so shiny and orderly. Jen was afraid to even sit on one of the seats.

But, of course, that was Meg. She and Jesse didn't call her Perfect Meg for nothing. Everything about her was that way. She was tall, thin, and well groomed. Before she had kids she'd worked in the development office of a bank. Now she was a stay-at-home mother who was vice president of the PTA, and spent most her waking hours running carpools. Meg was everything Adele Merriman wanted for her sons.

She was everything Jen wasn't.

"Mom, I'm hungry," Max announced as he wandered into the kitchen

Meg pulled her head out of the oven. "We're going to eat soon, Maxie," she assured her son.

"Not soon. NOW!" Max stamped his foot.

"A temper tantrum won't get you anywhere," Meg said calmly.

As if to prove her wrong, Max banged his fist on the table angrily. "Now! Now! Now!"

Jen winced. Meg's body language was clearly angry—all stiff and suddenly cold. She was afraid Perfect Meg was going to become un-Perfect for a moment, and maybe even . . . gasp! . . . let out some emotion.

But no such luck. Instead, Meg walked over to the fridge, pulled out three carrot sticks, and handed them to Max. "A little healthy snack couldn't hurt," she told Jen with a shrug.

At just that moment, Casper, the family cocker spaniel, came running into the kitchen. He barked at Max and jumped up high, trying to grab one of the carrot sticks. But Max wasn't giving in. He simply stuck out his tongue at the dog and walked back into the family room.

Casper padded around the kitchen a while longer, obviously intrigued by the smell of fresh food. He looked so hungry, Jen felt bad for him. She stood up, went over to the counter, and pulled a piece of sausage out of the bowl of stuffing. She held out her hand, and Casper came running over.

"Oh, for goodness' sake, Jen, not people food." Meg sighed, exasperated. "He's got to eat his own food. Otherwise, he'll become a complete beggar. They only behave the way they've been taught to."

Jen frowned, wondering how Max had learned to behave the way *he* did, but said nothing. Instead, she busied herself tossing the salad.

Suddenly, the doorbell rang. Meg leaped to attention and hurried for the door. "That must be Mike and Ellie," she told Jen.

"Who?"

"My side of the family," Meg explained. "Mike's my cousin. They have a seven-year-old son, Austin. He's a bit of a whiner, but Samantha and Max seem to like him."

Jen followed Perfect Megan into the family room and waited as she opened the door and gave kisses to her family. Mike and Ellie greeted Jesse, Richie, Adele, and Sam similarly. When they got to Jennifer, they stopped.

"Oh, that's right, you don't know our Jennifer," Adele said, using the word "our" a bit disingenuously. "She's Jesse's new bride."

"So nice to meet you," Ellie said.

"Glad to have some fresh blood at the Thanksgiving table," Mike added.

Austin didn't say anything. He was too busy playing with his handheld video game to even look up.

"Can I try that?" Max asked his cousin.

Austin shook his head.

"Now, Aussie," Ellie began.

"I don't feel like it!"

"Hey, big guy, how about we make a deal?" Mike suggested to his son. "When you reach level six, you'll give Max a turn."

Austin frowned. "How about level eight? That's the one where I shoot all the red devils in the cave."

"Okay, fair enough," Mike agreed.

Ellie turned to Megan. "We're trying to give him ownership of his decisions. Since we negotiated with Austin, he feels as though he was in on the decision. That way, he's more likely to actually go through with sharing."

"Interesting life lesson," Meg said.

Jennifer rolled her eyes. *They should just take the damn toy away from the spoiled brat.*

Just then, Casper came running up. He leaped up on Austin and tried to lick him in the face.

"AAAAHHHHHH!" Austin cried out. "GET IT AWAY."

"He's going through a fear-of-dogs phase," Ellie explained.

Austin's screams terrified Casper. He began barking wildly at the boy. Austin jumped up and grabbed his mom. In doing so, he dropped his handheld game. It fell to the floor with a crash. The batteries popped out.

That caught Casper's attention. He raced over and sniffed at the toy. "No, boy," Richie said as he yanked the cocker spaniel away from the batteries by the collar.

"I hate that dog!" Austin shouted.

"Hate is a strong word," Ellie said, trying to calm him. "How about saying, 'The dog makes me nervous'?"

"He won't hurt you," Samantha told Austin. "He just wanted to lick you."

"I hate him!" Austin repeated.

"I'll lock him in my bedroom," Meg told Ellie and Mike.

"That's not fair," Samantha argued. "It's

Thanksgiving. You're supposed to be with family on Thanksgiving. Now Casper can't be with us."

"Just because of dumb old Austin," Max added.

"I am not DUMB!" Austin told him.

Casper barked and jumped around as Richie held his collar.

Jen walked away from the screaming and barking. It was just too much to take.

A few minutes later, peace had been returned to the house. Casper, or *Cujo*, as Jen had taken to calling him privately, had been banished to Meg and Dave's bedroom. Mike had fixed Austin's video game, and the boy was sitting quietly at the table, happily shooting red devils and yellow demons while everyone else passed the potatoes and poured gravy over Meg's perfectly cooked turkey.

"Oh, this is delicious, Megan," Adele praised her. "The skin is so crispy." She turned to Jen. "Are you sure you won't try just a little bit? Our Meg here worked so hard on the turkey."

Jen pushed the mashed potatoes and broccoli around on her plate. "I'm sure it's delicious."

"Mom, I've told you a hundred times, Jen's a vegetarian," Jesse said, coming to her rescue.

"But it's Thanksgiving . . . ," Adele began.

"The turkey had nothing to be thankful for," Jen murmured under her breath, so low that only Jesse could hear.

Meg looked at Jennifer. "So how's school going?" she asked, trying to change the subject.

Jennifer smiled back gratefully. Sometimes it paid to have a sister-in-law who had perfect social skills. "Okay, I guess. I have finals and just one more semester."

"Then she enters the big, bad working world—" Jesse said proudly.

"*If* she can find work," Jesse's mother butted in.

"Adele . . . ," Sam Merriman warned.

"I just meant that the art field is so difficult to break into," Adele began. "Especially in New Jersey."

"Jen will probably be looking for work in the city," Jesse told his mom.

"Isn't that a big commute?" Adele asked. "You live at least forty-five minutes away by car. That's a lot of travel time."

"Jesse travels every day," Jen reminded her.

"Well, maybe we'll move to the city," Jesse told his mother. "Once Jen's done with school, we don't have to stay in New Jersey. We're only here now so she can get a New Jersey residency break on her tuition."

"Move to the city?" Adele gasped. "How can you expect to raise children in the city?"

"Who said anything about children?" Jesse asked.

"I actually like city kids," Jen told Adele. "They're sophisticated, and well schooled. Their playgrounds are the museums, galleries, shops, and concert halls. That's a lot more interesting than spending weekends at the malls."

"I don't think growing up in the city is a good thing," Ellie countered. "Children need room to run. Now take Austin here. He plays soccer, Little League, and he does tae kwon do. Could he do all that in the city?"

"I don't see why not," Jen replied. "There's Central Park, and plenty of dojos in the city."

"Doesn't Austin have any time to just go out and play?" Meg asked Ellie.

"No. I prefer structure," Ellie replied. "Children thrive on schedules. Random play-time just throws them off."

The conversation began to swirl around Jen. People were arguing about their philosophies for raising kids. Suddenly her head began to ache. Her stomach felt a little queasy. "Excuse me," she said quietly as she stood up and headed for the bathroom.

Jen had been gone quite awhile when Jesse finally excused himself from the table to look for her. The others had been so involved in their child-rearing argument that they hadn't noticed her absence. But Jesse sure had. He went upstairs and checked for her in the various bedrooms. But she was nowhere to be found. "Jen?" he called out.

"In here." Her voice sounded small and tired. It was coming from the bathroom.

"Can I come in?"

"Sure, it's open. They're all open. There are no locks on these doors."

Jesse laughed as he walked into the bathroom. "I'm sure it's some weird thing about wanting your kids to know you're always open to them." He laughed. "If I ever become like those people, I give you full permission to give me electroshock therapy." He looked down at the tile floor where Jen was sitting cross-legged, leaning against the wall. "Are you okay?"

"I just felt a little queasy," she said. "Too much stimulation, I guess."

"I'm with you. My family can definitely be a bit much."

"Just a bit," Jen said. "I wanted a little quiet, is all."

"Are you sick?"

"Just stressed."

Jesse stood up and shut the door. "I know what you need," he told her. "The best way to relax is to take a hot bath." He reached over and turned on the faucet in the tub.

"You want me to take a bath, right now, in the middle of Thanksgiving dinner?" Jen was very surprised. But she immediately whipped her pink sweater off over her head.

Jesse nodded. Then he began to unbutton his shirt, as well. "You know, I'm kind of stressed too," he said as he reached over and poured a little of Samantha and Max's bubble bath into the water. Foamy white bubbles immediately began to cover the surface.

"Mmm . . . bubbles." Jen sighed as she took off her pants and gingerly stepped into the tub, which was quickly filling up. She smiled at her husband as she bent down and splashed a few bubbles on her body. "Come on in," she told him. "The water's fine."

The sight of Jen completely naked, rubbing soapy water on her body, was just about all Jesse could handle. He stepped into tub and pulled her down into the water with him. He pressed her back against the back of the tub and began kissing her wildly. Jen kissed him back with equal pressure, and then gently began massaging his back, rubbing the warm sudsy water around in gentle circles, reaching lower and lower, until her slippery hands were circling his butt.

"Jen, you're so amazing," he whispered as he nibbled on her neck, slowly lowering his lips onto her collarbone, the top of her chest, her breasts.

"Oh, yeah." Jen moaned slightly. Lifting her hips slightly, letting him know that it was all right to . . .

"AAAAHHHHHHHHHHHHHHHHH!" Suddenly a child's voice filled the air. Jen and Jesse looked up to see Austin standing over them, screaming.

"Oh my God!" Jen cried out, burying herself under the bubbles.

"Austin, get the hell out of here!" Jesse shouted to the boy. He reached up his hand and pulled the shower curtain shut.

But it was too late. Austin had already gotten an eyeful. "MOMMMMMMMYYYYYYY!" he cried as he raced back downstairs. "Jesse's taking a bath with that brown-haired girl! They're both NAKED!!"

Jennifer was not looking forward to going back to the others. It was only after Jesse promised her that they could leave right away that she managed to get dressed and go downstairs to face the inquisition.

The adults were gathered in the living room when Jen and Jesse came downstairs. Adele was downing another vodka Gimlet. Megan was trying to calm Ellie. Mike and Richie were watching the football game with Sam. Obviously the kids had been shooed off to the basement playroom—out of the way of the evildoers of the bathtub.

"How could you?" Ellie demanded of Jesse and Jen as they entered the room. "He's just a little boy."

"Hell, we don't even take the kid to PG movies," Mike called from the couch. "Guess now we don't have to."

Ellie was not amused by her husband's jocularity. She stared angrily at the newlyweds. "You've probably scarred him for life. I hope you realize what a nightmare this is for him."

That was more than Jen could take. "*We* scarred him?" she shouted accusingly at Ellie. "Frankly, I'd rather have my child see two people making love than allow him to spend all day killing people on a video game."

The room went silent. For a moment, no one said anything. Then Jesse walked over and wrapped his arm around Jen. "What Austin saw was beautiful and natural," he added in agreement with his wife. "But you guys probably haven't tried it recently enough to remember."

"Now, Jesse, don't be base," his mother scolded him.

"It's not base, Mom. Richie, if you and Meg had locks on your doors, this never would have happened."

"I don't lock my children out of my life," Perfect Meg explained.

Jen bit back a laugh. *Just as Jesse had predicted.*

"You know what, guys?" Jesse continued. "I have to thank you. You made me see that I'm not ready to be a parent yet. Or maybe at all. I'm not sure I'll ever be ready to listen to whiny kids fighting over violent games, having temper tantrums while begging for food, or bursting into rooms without knocking, which is just plain rude. In fact, I think you should consider having your kids all become models. They'd be great poster children for Planned Parenthood!"

With that, he grabbed his coat and headed out the door, leaving the others to stare at his back as he left.

Jen didn't know what to say. There was no way to follow that performance. So all she said was, "Bye. Happy Thanksgiving. Enjoy the cheesecake."

Wow! Jesse really blew me away today. I never thought he could tell his family off the way he did. Up till now, he's just sort of ignored them, letting them say what they wanted without getting involved. But today, he stood up for himself—and for me. It couldn't have been easy, but he did it. I'm so proud of my husband. He's my hero.

Still, I kind of wish those kids hadn't been so damned awful today. It's just going to make what I have to tell him that much harder.

Longer letter later.

—Jen

I Have to Pee on *What*?!

"Jesse, I think I'm pregnant."

The words sat there in the air for a moment, not really reaching Jesse's ears. Or at least not his conscious mind. It took a minute for them to register there.

"But you can't be . . . ," he began finally. "It's not possible."

"Maybe not, but I think I am," Jen replied.

He looked at her. "You're on the Pill. It's foolproof."

"Yeah, well, that's sort of the problem," Jen began slowly. "The Pill's only foolproof if you remember to take it every day."

"And you didn't?"

"I thought I did, but at the end of the month

I had two Pills left over. There must have been a time when I forgot or something and . . ."

Jesse's head was reeling now. He wanted to scream, freak out. He wanted to tell her he couldn't believe she'd been so careless. But he couldn't. It was probably almost as much his fault as it was hers. Hell, he'd been the one to leave the birth control in her court. He hadn't exactly been bringing home condoms for them to use. Once he and Jen had both been tested for HIV and had come up negative, they'd never bothered with condoms again. They were in a committed relationship. *Safe.* And with Jen on the Pill, he figured they were safe from pregnancy, too. Apparently that wasn't so.

But, looking into Jen's huge blue eyes, he just couldn't be angry with her. She seemed so frightened. Who knew how long she'd been keeping this to herself, afraid to tell him? "How late are you?" he asked her, pulling himself together for her sake.

"About a week."

Jesse felt his entire body relax. "Oh, is that all? Well, that doesn't mean anything. It's easy to be a week late and still not be . . . I mean isn't it?"

Jen shrugged. "I guess. It's just that I'm

always so regular. And I've been having all these weird symptoms. Like at your sister's house yesterday, when I had to get up to leave the table, I was feeling kind of nauseous."

"But that could have been smell of the turkey. Or my family. They have that affect on a lot of people." *That's it, Jesse,* he thought. *Add a little levity to the situation.*

But Jen wasn't in a humorous mood. She was scared to death. "I don't think that was it."

And then the realization hit him: She hadn't been drinking yesterday at the Thanksgiving party. He hadn't thought about it at the time, but she'd turned down one of Richie's special martinis. Which could mean only one thing. *She already knew.* "You took the test already, didn't you?" he accused her.

Jen shook her head. "I bought one, but I can't bring myself to do it."

"Well, you've got to, Jen. If you are—" he stumbled over the word for a moment "—*pregnant,* then we have to find a doctor and start taking care of you and the baby."

They stared at each other for a moment. *Baby.* For such a small creature, it was an incredibly powerful word.

"I can't," Jen told him in a small voice. "I'm too scared."

"Come on, we can do this."

Jen looked at him strangely. "*We?* I'm the one who's got to pee on that stick. I'm the one who has to get all fat, and give up college, move to the suburbs, wear tacky high-waist jeans, drive carpools to soccer practice and cub scouts, put child-proof gadgets on all the cabinets, get a dog and—"

"Whoa, take it easy," Jesse said, pulling her close and holding her till she calmed down. "You're jumping ahead of yourself. None of that has to happen."

"Oh, I won't have to get fat?"

Jesse laughed in spite of himself. "Okay, maybe *that* has to happen. But the rest of it? No way. Who says you have to give up college? Even if you are pregnant, you'll be able to graduate before the baby is born. And after graduation, you can still get a job. There's always day care or baby-sitters. And we can even move to the city and raise a kid there. You're not my sister-in-law or her wacky cousin. And I'm not those uptight golfing guys in my office. We're us. Jen and Jesse. We can do this our way. We're a team."

Jen nodded slowly, taking it all in. "It's true," she admitted. "We are different."

"We could raise a pretty cool kid," Jesse agreed. "One that *likes* being different."

"And at least we'll be young enough to enjoy her . . . or him," Jen began. "I mean, if you have a kid when you're forty, it's pretty tough to run with a bicycle, or go hiking with her. And who wants to put up with a kid in puberty when your own hormones are going crazy with menopause." Jen shuddered for a minute. "Okay, I don't want to think about having a teenager. If my kid is anything like I was . . . look out!"

Jesse laughed. He could only imagine what Jen was like then. "Look, could you not rush our whole lives, please? I can't believe you're thinking about being middle-aged. You're twenty-one! I think you're going out of your mind."

"See? They say pregnant women have mood swings. Maybe this is a mood swing!" Jen sounded really panicked now.

"Look, this whole discussion may be for nothing," Jesse reminded her, trying to keep his cool, and hoping his calmness would rub off of Jen. "You don't know for sure if you're pregnant."

Jen couldn't argue with that. "The test is in my backpack. I guess I could take it, and then—"

"We'll deal with *then*, later."

Jesse watched as Jen went into the bedroom in search of the pregnancy test. Alone there in the room, he realized for the first time that his heart was beating slightly harder, and his palms were sweating. He'd been working so hard at appearing calm for Jen that he hadn't realized that he wasn't really calm at all.

A baby. Well, that would definitely change everything. More bills, more stress. More responsibility. Hell, he was only twenty-three. And at twenty-one Jen was just barely legal. Weren't they supposed to have a few more years of fun?

On the other hand, it wasn't like they *weren't* planning on having kids someday. It had just come a little sooner than they'd anticipated. And raising a kid with Jen could be fun. Like on snowy days, they could all go outside, the three of them, the family, and build snowmen in the park. With all her craft skills, Jen could help the kid with school projects, and Jesse could coach ice hockey. It would be kind of cool to have a little boy he could teach to skate.

If the kid was a girl, Jesse could go to her ballet recitals, or her music performances. She could be Daddy's little girl. A carbon copy of her mom, with big eyes and long dark hair. He'd protect her from all the bad boys out there—bad boys like Dave, the musician her mother had dated—

"Okay, I've got it," Jen interrupted his thoughts as she walked in the living room carrying a lavender and white cardboard box in her hand.

"Do you know what to do?"

Jen nodded. "I looked at the directions. I'm supposed to pee on the stick, and then wait to see if the little window turns pink. It takes about five minutes for the results to show up."

"Okay," Jesse said. "Go ahead."

"Aren't you coming with me?"

"While you pee on a stick?"

Jen shrugged. "I thought we were in this together. Come on, Jesse. I'm kind of scared."

So Jesse followed his wife into the bathroom and sat on the tub while she peed on the long white stick.

"Okay, nothing to do but wait," Jen said, placing the stick on the sink and staring at the empty white window in the wide end.

"I'm checking my watch," Jesse assured her. He lifted his wrist and lowered his eyes, watching each second tick by. "Good thing this one is so accurate. You know, I paid extra to make sure it was an extremely accurate timepiece. It runs on a special kind of battery that—"

"Jesse," Jen interrupted.

"What?"

"Could we not talk about watches?"

Jesse nodded. Instead, he stood up and moved beside her.

They stood there in silence, each staring at the stick, each lost in his and her own thoughts.

"How long has it been?" Jen asked him after it seemed they had been standing like that for a very long time.

"About a minute and a half," Jesse answered.

"Oh. I thought it had been a lot longer."

"I know what you mean."

"I never realized five minutes was such a long time. I mean, it doesn't seem like a long time when you've got five minutes left to finish your exam, or five minutes left in a really good movie or something," Jen said. "So how come it seems so long when you're trying to find out if

. . . if . . ." She looked up at him. "How are we going to do this?"

"We will," he assured her. "I'm not sure how. We just will. Just promise me one thing."

"What?"

"Careen will not be our baby's godmother."

"Only if you keep Artie out of the godfather job," Jen told him.

"Deal."

"And I definitely don't want Perfect Megan and Richie being the godparents either." Jen shuddered at the thought. "Can you imagine?"

Jesse grimaced. "I've got a great idea," he said. "We won't have godparents for our baby. We'll be renegades. Break with tradition."

"Sounds good to me," Jen said, squeezing his hand. Then she laughed. "Fatherhood is changing you already. Imagine you—Mr. Safe and Accurate—as a renegade."

"Hey, I'm not so safe," Jesse teased.

"Sure you are."

"No, I'm not. If I always played it safe, we wouldn't be standing here, staring at this stick, waiting for it to turn pink."

Jen couldn't argue with that one. "How much longer now?" she asked him.

"Another thirty seconds." He looked down at the stick. "It hasn't changed at all yet."

Jen looked down. "Maybe the color appears at the very end," she suggested.

Jesse didn't answer. Instead, he looked back down at his watch, checking as each second clicked by. Finally, he looked up. "Okay, that's five minutes."

They looked down at the stick. The window was still white.

"Well, that's that," Jen said. "I guess I'm not pregnant."

"Yeah," Jesse replied.

"We lucked out, huh?" Jen asked him quietly.

"Yeah. Lucked out," Jess repeated.

"I guess it was just stress, or missing a day or two of the Pill or something," Jen continued. "I must have thrown my cycle off."

"Mmm-hmm," Jesse murmured. He continued staring at the blank window in the middle of the stick.

"Well, then, I think I'll go have a glass of wine," Jen said, throwing the stick in the trash. "I can have one now."

Jesse nodded. "Get me one too."

Jen turned and started out the door. Suddenly

she stopped and looked to Jesse. "How come I feel I lost something really special?" she asked him.

"I know what you mean."

A pregnancy scare. *I've heard about them before. Friends of mine have had them. And some of them weren't just scares. Some of them were actual pregnancies. And that left my friends with pretty heavy decisions to make. You know, whether to keep the baby, or put it up for adoption, or just end the pregnancy.*

Of course, of my friends who've been pregnant, none of them were married. And as I have just learned, having a supportive partner you can trust to stick by you makes all the difference. If I had been pregnant, Jesse and I would have been partners in raising the kid. We would have done it together.

There's no question we would have taken the pregnancy full term. We both want kids, and even though this wouldn't have been the right time, you can't always choose. My mother always tells me that if people waited until they were ready to have babies to have

them, there would never be anybody born.
You just have to close your eyes and jump
right in.

  Sort of like marriage, I guess.
—Jen

Cheep . . . Cheep . . . Cheap!!!!

Jen lifted her head and took a good strong whiff. She loved the smell of New York City in the winter. The scent of the hot chestnuts wafting from the vendor's cart, mixing with the cold air coming off the ice-skating rink, was pure heaven.

Of course, Jen loved New York any time of the year. She remembered begging her parents to drive her the nearly one and a half hours into the city almost all the time when she was a kid. And usually, they'd obliged.

Jen's parents weren't huge fans of the city— they far preferred their little artsy neighborhood in New Jersey. But from time to time they would make the journey over the bridge on Jen's behalf, usually going to the Village for the annual Labor Day art show, or heading in to visit a gallery or see a performance by one of their friends who might have been lucky enough to get a gig in the city.

In Jen's small New Jersey hometown, lots of the other families thought Jen and her parents were crazy. They had a genuine fear of New York City, often going on and on about the crowds, the prices, the parking, the pickpockets, and, of course, the murders on the subway. Jen's parents didn't entirely disagree with them, but they did try to give Jen a chance to make up her own mind about the place.

The strategy had served to make Jen love the Big Apple. Jen was never afraid in New York. She loved the rhythm of the place—whether it was the offbeat movement of the Greenwich Villagers, or the fast-paced *click-clicking* of the well-heeled residents of the Upper East Side. She adored Central Park, and the Metropolitan Museum of Art. It was her dream to get Jesse to love the city as much as she did.

Which was part of the reason she had dragged him into the city today. She was in the mood to celebrate. Finals were over, and she'd managed to pull off some pretty good grades—

even in that dreaded Nietzsche class. She deserved to go wild. And there was no better place to do that than in the city.

"Wow! Look at the tree!" Jesse exclaimed as they walked into Rockefeller Center. The giant Christmas tree had just been erected. It was huge and full. The smell of pine seemed to permeate the air. Best of all, it was lit up with thousands of multi-color lights. "I think it's even bigger than last year's! I don't think I've ever seen any tree that big."

"Makes me kind of sad they had to chop it down, though," Jen admitted. "Imagine how many years it lived to get to that size. It was probably alive when our great-grandparents were, you know?"

Jesse didn't answer. There'd be no winning an environmental battle with his Greenpeace-loving, tree-hugging wife. Better to change the subject. "You ready to skate?"

Jen nodded. "I guess so. But you're going to have to help me. I haven't been on the ice in a really long time."

"Good. After a whole day of going to museums and looking at art, there's finally something I'll be able to teach you!"

It was true. Jen had dragged Jesse through the Whitney Museum and the Guggenheim in an effort to get him to appreciate modern art the way she did. It hadn't been a completely successful endeavor, but at least he'd tried.

Which was exactly what Jen was doing right now on the ice-skating rink at Rockefeller Center. All around her people were skating, happily whirling around in circles, moving backward, and gliding in the most amazing ballet positions. But Jen was just trying to keep from falling. She moved her legs back and forth, trying to move along. To his credit, Jesse hadn't just skated off. He was there by her side, offering encouragement—and a whole lot of advice.

"Stop looking at the ice," he told her as he skated backward in front of her so that they could be face-to-face as they skated around. "Keep your head up and just glide."

"Easier said than done, my friend," Jen said, moving her feet as gracefully as she could— which wasn't particularly graceful at all.

"You're getting it," Jesse assured her.

Jen smiled. She knew he was lying, but he was being so damned sweet about it. And so she

kept on skating and, in truth, she did get a little better as the afternoon progressed. But after
a while, her ankles started to hurt. She was cold,
and tired, and she really wasn't having any fun.

She suspected Jesse wasn't having a great
time either. He was used to being free on the
ice—gliding around, feeling the wind in his
face. He always came home from the pickup
ice-hockey games he played on Tuesday nights
feeling fresh and alive. Jesse was at home on the
ice. And there was no way he was getting that
kind of rush baby-sitting Jen while she trudged
away, skating slowly around the outer rim of the
rink, grabbing on to the wall for support when
she felt like she was about to fall.

"I'm going to call it quits," she finally told
him. "Get a hot chocolate or something in that
coffeeshop we saw earlier."

"Oh, okay," Jesse said, sounding only slightly
disappointed. "We can stop now."

"No, you don't have to stop," she assured
him. "Go ahead and skate for a while. Have
fun."

Jesse didn't argue. Instead, he checked his
ever-present watch. "How about I meet you in
the coffeeshop at five-thirty?" he suggested.

"Great!" Jen agreed. "That gives me about half an hour to warm up before dinner."

As Jesse skated off and joined the mass of more expert skaters in the center of the ice, Jen went and changed out of her skates. On her way to the coffeeshop, she noticed a street vendor selling pocketbooks from a table. She walked over to take a look.

Jen knew the bags had to be fakes—imitations of real bags by designers like Kate Spade, Prada, and Louis Vuitton. But it was amazing how real they looked. She picked up one especially colorful Kate Spade handbag. "How much?"

"Twenty dollars," the man said, barely looking up. "They're all twenty dollars."

"Ooh," Jen said excitedly. "The Louis Vuitton, too?"

"All of them."

"Okay, I'll take this Kate Spade and the brown Louis Vuitton." She reached into her own little leather bag and pulled out two twenty-dollar bills. In exchange, the man handed her the two pocketbooks. "Do you have a shopping bag I can put these in?"

Finally, the man looked up. He stared at Jen

in surprise. "A shopping bag? No. Whaddaya want for twenty dollars? Maybe one of those big brown bags from Bloomingdale's?"

"Gosh, you don't have to be nasty about it," Jen said, taking her two purchases and walking away.

At five-thirty sharp, Jesse walked into the coffeeshop. Sure enough, Jen was there, sitting at the counter, finishing her hot chocolate. She looked up as he came in, smiled, and waved him over. "You look happy," she said as Jesse walked over and stood behind him.

"It was a good workout," he told her.

"At least the last half hour," she teased.

Jesse shook his head. "I loved skating with you."

"I love that you said that," Jen assured him. "But you're a lousy liar."

Jesse laughed. There was no fooling her. "How can you tell?"

"It's your eyebrows."

"My what?"

Jen pointed to the thick, straw-blond brows that framed his deep-set chocolate-brown eyes. "Your eyebrows. Whenever you're lying, you raise them just a tiny bit."

"I do not."

"You do," Jen assured him.

"Come on. That's ridiculous. Besides, I never lie to you," Jesse insisted.

"There they go again," Jen teased. "Hey, you want a hot chocolate?"

"Actually, I want some food," Jesse replied. "You know any cheap place to eat around here?"

"Around Rockefeller Center?" Jen asked him. "No way. 'Cheap' is not part of the vocabulary in this part of town. But I do know an amazing Spanish place down on Bleeker Street, in the West Village. You can get a one-and-a-half-pound lobster for fifteen dollars!"

"Yeah, but it'll cost me twenty dollars to park the car in a garage down there. We were pretty lucky to get a spot on the street up here," Jesse reminded her. "And don't forget how long it'll take us to drive down to the Village in this traffic. Maybe we should just go home and call in for pizza or something."

"Come on, Jesse," Jen moaned. She wasn't at all ready to leave the city just yet. "We could take the subway down to the Village, and then after dinner come back up for the car."

"The *subway*?" Jesse's voice scaled up nervously. "I don't like underground trains, Jen. They make me feel claustrophobic. You're trapped down there with all these strange people and—

"Strange? Define *strange*."

"Just people I don't know, I guess," Jesse replied. *"Strangers."*

"Well, by that definition, *you're* strange. So am I—at least to the other people on the train."

Jesse considered that for a moment. It was hard to argue her point. Still . . . "I hate the subway," he told her.

"Oh, you're just chicken."

"I am not."

"Cheep . . . cheep . . . chicken!" Jen repeated. She moved her arms up and down like wings.

"Oh yeah?" Jesse replied. "Fine. I'll show you who's chicken. Last one to the Number One train is a rotten egg." And with that, he started off toward the door.

"Wait, Jesse, I have to pay for this cocoa. You have any money?"

"I gave you forty dollars when we left the house," Jesse reminded her. "I stopped at the bank, remember?"

"Yeah, but I already spent that."

Jesse looked at her strangely. "How much did you eat here?"

"Oh, I didn't eat. I just had the cocoa. I spent the money on these." She reached down and picked up the two pocketbooks. "Aren't they adorable? And can you believe it—they were only twenty dollars each!"

Jesse looked at the two bags. "I believe it," he assured her. "Jen, these are fakes."

"Of course they are. You can't buy the real ones on the street."

Jesse shook his head in disbelief. "You bought these from some guy on the street? Are you nuts?"

"What's wrong with buying things on the street?"

"People sell crap on the streets. These are going to fall apart in like a week."

Jen's eyes grew small and angry. A fresh pink tone rose up in her cheeks. "I sell plenty of jewelry on the streets, at fairs and things. Are you saying my jewelry is crap?"

"That's not what I said, and you know it," Jesse told her. Then, noticing that people were staring at them, he threw three dollars on the counter and quickly ushered her out of the coffeeshop.

"I can't believe you're mad over a lousy forty dollars," she said as they walked out into the cold.

"I can't believe you spent it," he replied. "You know I work hard for that money."

"Jesse, you need to break free. Chill out. Maybe *you* should go on a shopping spree sometime."

"I did. I bought that new drill just last week."

"Going to a hardware store isn't shopping."

"It is to me. It is to any man. Take a poll."

"Fine," Jen agreed. She walked over to a heavyset man in a black down parka. "Excuse me, sir," she said, and stopped him. "Do you consider going to the hardware store a shopping spree?"

The man stared at her peculiarly and then continued walking down the street, picking up his pace a bit.

"What do you think you're doing?" Jesse asked her.

"Taking a poll, just like you said." She started walking over to a father who was heading toward the ice-skating rink with his two sons.

"All right, cut it out," Jesse told her. "You're not funny."

"I'm not trying to be funny," Jen replied. "I just don't understand what the big deal is about forty dollars."

"Maybe that's because you've never worked for that forty dollars," Jesse spat out. The blood rushed to his face. He realized immediately that he shouldn't have said that. "I didn't mean that, that way," he added feebly.

"Yes you did," Jen told him. "You meant it. You always mean it. Sooner or later it always comes back to the same thing: You're working, and I'm not. Well, how many times do I have to tell you, I can't work. I'm in school!"

"I worked when I was in school. I had three internships before I graduated. That's how I got a real job *when* I graduated." Jesse was shouting now. "I don't see why you can't at least *start* looking for some sort of job now. Maybe working at a publishing house that makes those arty coffee table books or—"

"For heaven's sake, a publishing house? Why would I want to do something like that?" Jen groaned.

"Because it's a job. A *real* job," he insisted. "In

an office, with a regular salary, and benefits. Something we can count on in our monthly budget."

"Salary. Benefits. Budget. Will you listen to yourself, Jesse? You sound like some old man. Like those uptight golfing guys you work with." Jen frowned. "Well, what if I told you I don't want a real job? At least not what *you* consider real."

Jesse stared at her, surprised. The thought that Jen might not want to work after graduation had never occurred to him. "What happened to your big career in the art world?"

"*I* never said I wanted that," Jen reminded him. "That was something you and your mother convinced yourselves of."

"But . . . but . . . ," Jesse stammered. "Where is this coming from, Jen?"

She stopped for a minute and looked at him. He looked cartoonishly deranged, as if steam were about to come out his ears like one of those animated characters in the old Looney Toons shorts.

She realized that maybe she'd gone too far. Maybe she'd made him think that she intended on having him support her for the rest of her life, like *Megan* or someone. But that hadn't been what she'd meant at all. She could never be like that. "I'm going to work, Jesse," she assured him. "Just not in that kind of job. Maybe teach yoga somewhere, and make jewelry. I could give tours at art museums. Do all sorts of things. I mean, come on. Can you see me in an office? I'd spend the whole time wondering what gave anyone the right to tell me I had to be in that building between the hours of nine and five."

"They *pay* for that right," Jesse told her. "It's called a salary."

"It's called *indentured servitude*," Jen corrected him. "That's what you're under. When the people in your office say jump, you jump. In fact, you ask how high and through which hoop."

"I have to do that."

"Why?"

"Because I have a wife who buys crappy pocketbooks on the street, wants lobster for dinner, and has decided to teach yoga for a living!" Jesse shouted back at her.

Jen stared at him for a minute. She didn't like it when he yelled. She hated the idea of him being angry with her. Not that she wasn't a little angry with him, too. But she didn't want to fight. Not here. In her favorite city. *Not right in front of the Christmas tree.*

"Look, why don't we just go home and have leftovers?" Jen suggested finally. "We can save thirty dollars by not having the lobster." Her voice was small. She sounded contrite, even a little scared.

Jesse picked up on the tone of her voice. "No. We'll go downtown," he said, obviously as anxious to put this fight behind them as she was. "This is your end-of-semester celebration. We should do what you want to do."

Jen studied his face. "You mean it?"

Jesse nodded. "I mean it." He pointed up to his forehead. "See? No raised eyebrows."

Jen giggled with relief. The tension had passed. She kissed him on his cold, red nose and then turned and headed toward the subway station. "Last one to the train is a rotten egg!"

I hate fighting with Jen. It just takes it all out of me. But sometimes she makes me so mad. She just won't grow up. She's like some sort of female Peter Pan who thinks life is going to be one long, undergrad experience. You know, classes, parties, and hanging out. She doesn't realize once you get out of school, you have to pay your own way. No more student loans or work-study projects to bail you out. You've got to find a way to pay for the rent and the utility bills, and even for the cute little pocketbooks you find on the street. You have to take responsibility. *I know Jen hates that word—along with other words like "budget," "salary," and "balanced checkbook." But that's a part of life. And as much as my beautiful, creative wife would like to think that she and I live in our own private universe, a place where life is all about happiness, art, beautiful music, and good sex, the truth is, we don't live in some sort of incredible Utopia that's just for me and Jen. We live in the real world. And in the real world, sooner or later you've got to get a real job.*

But hey. She's got a whole semester of school to figure that out. In the meantime, I'm going to try and relax a little about the whole money thing.

Oh yeah. Right. Who am I kidding?

—Jesse

That's Why Bachelor Parties Are for Bachelors!

"Now Jen, please try to be nice," Jesse urged as he threw on the blue crewneck sweater Jen had knitted him for Christmas. "Remember, he's my best friend. And Felicia's the first girl he's ever really fallen for. I think it's nice that they like going out to dinner with us."

"It is," Jen assured him. "And I do like Felicia. She's smart and sweet. A real gentle soul. She'd never say a mean thing about anyone. Which leads to the obvious question: What could someone like that possibly see in *Artie*?"

"That's what I'm talking about," Jesse pointed out. "Be nice."

Jen looked down at the three sweaters she'd

laid out on the bed. "Which one should I wear?" she asked him.

"Don't ask me."

Jen sighed and struggled to fasten her black lacy bra behind her. "I wasn't trying to be mean. I was just wondering what Felicia sees in Artie that I don't."

"She thinks he's fascinating," Jesse said, and shrugged.

"Oh, so *that's* what they have in common," Jen teased.

"What?"

"They both think Artie's fascinating."

Jesse had to laugh at that one. Jen laughed too—that rich, hearty laugh that rang out like bells. He watched as she slipped on a tight fuzzy black and red sweater. It was just low cut enough to give a good view of her considerable cleavage—sexy without being too showy. Just like Jen. Jesse couldn't help himself. He reached out and grabbed his wife, throwing her onto the bed.

"Oh, you big strong man." Jen giggled as he ran his hands up her sweater and began to unhook the bra she'd just struggled to fasten.

"Me man, you woman," Jesse grunted back in his best caveman voice.

"Glad you've got the biology down," Jen teased. She reached over and unbuttoned his jeans. "Oh, I see *you* won't need any encouragement," she laughed, looking down.

"I never do," Jesse assured her, helping her slip out of her own jeans.

"Aren't we going to be late?" Jen murmured.

But for once, Jesse didn't care about the time. All he could think about was the two of them, here and now. "Shut up," he teased her.

"Make me."

As if to prove that he could, Jesse placed his mouth on hers and opened his lips, letting his tongue find hers. Her arms reached out and gripped his back, pulling him toward her. They began to move in an intimate dance, twisting and turning their mouths, their tongues, their hands, their bodies, and their legs, all in unison, until at last they were completely intertwined.

"Sorry we're late," Jesse said as he and Jen met up with Artie and Felicia in the restaurant. "Jen had a little trouble picking out clothes."

Jen blushed slightly.

"From the sudden rise of red in your wife's

pallor, I'd say she had less trouble getting *undressed* than dressed," Artie teased.

Jen blushed harder.

"Oh, Artie, you're so funny," Felicia gushed.

"A riot," Jen murmured under her breath.

"Well, I suppose you were wondering why we wanted to meet you two tonight," Artie said, suddenly sounding extremely businesslike.

"To eat?" Jesse joked.

"Well, that . . . and to tell you our grandiose news," Artie replied.

Felicia looked up at him with complete adoration in her eyes. It was obvious she hung on every word Artie said. Even the ones it was impossible to understand.

"We wanted to let you know that we're joining you by jumping into the matrimonial ring."

"You're what?" Jesse said. It was impossible for him to hide his surprise. After all, Artie and Felicia had only been dating about three months—even less than Jesse and Jen had been when they'd gotten engaged.

"We're getting married. Next month." Artie sounded pleased and proud.

"In a month?" Now it was Jen's turn to sound surprised. "What's the hurry?"

"No hurry," Artie said quickly. "We just decided not to wait."

Jen studied Artie's face. He seemed slightly nervous—the way lawyers do when they're lying. Obviously Artie had found the perfect field for himself. No doubt there was more to the story. And judging from the fact that Artie was drinking a beer while his bride-to-be was downing a bottle of Poland Spring, Jen was pretty sure she knew what that was. Obviously, Artie wasn't just going to be a husband. He was going to be a father, too.

Artie as a dad. That poor child.

"Well, that's just wonderful," Jen finally said. She smiled kindly at Felicia. "You're a lucky man, Artie."

"I'm lucky too," Felicia assured her. "Imagine, me marrying someone as bright and handsome as Artie."

"Mmm . . . ," Jen murmured. "How lucky."

Jesse gave her a slight nudge under the table. A warning that she'd promised to be nice.

"Well, there's another topic I'd like to broach with you, Jesse," Artie began.

"What? You want advice for the wedding night?" Jesse teased. "Don't you think you ought to be asking your father for that?"

"Oh, I have a feeling Artie's got that one mastered," Jen butted in, only to receive another warning nudge from Jesse.

"Actually, I wanted to request that you be my second on this endeavor."

"Your what?" Jesse said, genuinely confused.

"My second. My groomsman. The one who stands beside me as I take the plunge."

"Oh, you want me to be your best man," Jesse translated. "Wow. Thanks dude."

"It seems only fair, since I was your best man," Artie replied. "Now, Felicia and I don't have a sweet agreement with a Web site like Duets, so our wedding probably won't have all the little classic touches that yours did . . ."

"Don't worry about it," Jen said ruefully, remembering the details of her wedding day. The party favors—mints with the Duets logo on them. The cocktail napkins with the Web address on them. And all that cheesy eighties music. "I'm sure it will be lovely," Jen said. "You can plan a wedding that really reflects the two of you."

"Jen, I would have loved to ask you to be a bridesmaid," Felicia began nervously, "but I have three sisters and—"

"Oh don't be silly," Jen said with genuine relief. She'd been saved from having to wear a bridesmaid's dress chosen by Felicia. It was obvious the woman didn't have the greatest taste. If she had, she'd never have chosen to propagate the species with someone like Artie.

"Okay, so I'm sorry I didn't give you a lot of warning," Artie told Jesse.

"I'm not the one who needs warning," Jesse told him. "You're the ones who have to get the hall, the caterer, the music, the flowers . . ."

"Yes, but you're the one who has to plan the bachelor party," Artie reminded him. "Now, I don't want anything grandiose—just some of our fraternity brothers, maybe a few of the fellows in my law school. I have a list of e-mail addresses if you need them so you can send out the invitations. And I know that the firehouse in Jersey City sometimes rents out a room for things like these. Then there's the beer, of course, and the food. I think that deli near you delivers platters and kegs. And of course, we've got to have entertainment—"

"What *kind* of entertainment?" Jen interrupted suspiciously.

"Well, Jen, it is a bachelor party," Artie reminded her.

"So you mean strippers?" Jen asked accusingly.

"Well, not strippers necessarily . . ." Artie was becoming flustered. "But—"

"Because I know Jesse would never participate in an event in which women were put on display like that. Would you, Jesse?"

It wasn't really a question.

"Um . . . no, hon. Of course not." Jesse looked hopelessly at Artie.

"Jesse has respect for women," Jen continued. "I would hope for Felicia's sake that you do too. Would you want your sister, or your wife, or your daughter"—she stared pointedly at Felicia's stomach—"making a living taking off her clothes for a bunch of horny, leering guys?"

The table grew quiet for a moment, no one knowing quite what to say to that. Finally, it was Felicia who broke the silence. "I have to say I kind of agree with Jen on this one, Artie sweetheart." She sounded almost unsure, as though this was the first time she'd ever disagreed with him.

"Well, we don't have to have strippers. There are plenty of other ways to have a bachelor party. We could play poker. I'll get some really awesome cigars, some single-malt Scotch and—," Jesse began.

"Whatever you want to do," Artie interrupted, sounding incredibly disappointed. "I'm not supposed to plan this, after all. It's in your hands. I'm going to leave the whole thing up to you."

"So ya think Jesse's gonna come home from the party a total horndog after ogling all those naked women?" Careen asked about three weeks later as she and Jen hung out in J-squared's apartment while Jesse was at Artie's party. "Say, are they going to have one of those tacky giant cakes the strippers jump out of? That would be perfect for Artie's bachelor party!" She laughed heartily.

"It's not that kind of bachelor party," Jen assured her best friend.

"Oh, is there another kind?"

Jen rolled her eyes. "It's just a bunch of guys getting together, playing poker, smoking cigars, and getting drunk."

"Bill Clinton said he was smoking *his* cigars

too," Careen reminded her. "But those stogies served a whole other purpose."

"Come on. Don't be ridiculous. *Jesse* planned this party, remember. And he swore to me that all they were going to do was play poker."

"And you believed him?"

"Of course I believed him. Jesse and I don't lie to each other. We tell the truth. Honesty is what all good relationships are based on."

Careen sighed, but didn't argue with her. Instead, she mused, "Poker, cigars, and beer. Sounds like a pretty dull night to me."

"It's male bonding," Jen told her. "Everything guys do together sounds dull."

"Yeah, not like us." Careen laughed, noting the irony in Jen's statement. After all, it wasn't as though she and Jen were exactly out rocking the town. She leaned back on the couch and picked up the remote. "Oh look, a new reality show. Now there's something different."

Meanwhile, at the firehouse, Jesse, Artie, and the guys really *were* playing poker. And despite the fact that Artie was raking in the chips, he didn't seem particularly happy. "Give me three cards," he said to the dealer at his table.

"Three for the groom," the dealer, Mark—Artie's law school associate—replied as he dealt Artie three new cards for his hand.

But before Artie could even check to see how his new hand looked, there was an angry knock at the door. "Police!" a strong, deep woman's voice announced. "Don't anybody move!"

Two women in police uniforms burst into the room. "Gambling is illegal in this township," one of the women announced. "I'm afraid we're going to have to take you all in."

"What the . . ." Artie leaped up. He turned to Jesse. "This is bad. *Really bad.* I can't get arrested. I'll never be allowed to practice law. You and your damn poker night. You've not only ruined my bachelor party, you may have ruined my whole damned life!"

But Jesse didn't seem at all upset. "Look, why don't you girls just take a break? Relax. You want a beer?"

"Jesse, are you nuts?" Artie hissed in his ear. He turned to the police officers. "Officers, I apologize for my friend. He didn't mean to imply that you would ever drink while on duty."

"Whose party is this?" the smaller of the two policewomen, a busty redhead, asked.

"The party's for him," Jesse said, pointing to Artie. "He's getting married in a few days."

"Thanks a lot, Jesse," Artie moaned. "I'll get you for this."

The taller of the two policewomen reached onto her belt and took out a pair of handcuffs. "Sorry, sir, you'll have to wear these," she said as she brought Artie's hands behind his back and cuffed him.

Then, suddenly, she leaned in close to the groom-to-be and rubbed her body against his. As if out of nowhere, music began blasting from a CD player in the corner of the room. The two police officers started unbuttoning their blouses, making sure that each of their movements matched the beat of the music.

"Get ready for a really arresting development," the taller, well-built woman warned as she stepped out of her pants, revealing a blue G-string. She pushed Artie into a chair and then straddled herself on his lap.

"Oh, man, you really had me fooled," Artie told Jesse as the woman shimmied back and forth. "I can't believe you lied to Jen for me. You're a real pal, bro."

"I didn't lie to Jen," Jesse swore. "I told her we

were going to play poker and smoke cigars. Which we have been. I just didn't mention that there were going to be a few unexpected guests."

"You're right, you didn't lie, " Artie assured him as he watched the stripper stand up and began dancing with her partner. "No jury in the world could ever convict you."

Just then, Jesse felt something vibrating his pants pocket. He laughed for a minute, thinking about how that must have looked to the strippers. Then he realized that the vibration was a cell phone call from Jen. She was the only one who'd call Jesse this late on a Saturday night.

For a minute, he considered not picking up—but of course that would only make her more suspicious. So instead, he walked out into the parking lot, shutting the door behind him before picking up. "Hello," he said into the receiver, hoping Jen couldn't hear the music and shouts coming from within the building.

"Hey, Jesse, how's it going?" Jen asked him.

"Oh, fine."

"Are you winning?"

"Not me. It's Artie's night. He's really hot right now." Okay, that wasn't exactly a lie. Artie was just a different kind of hot from what Jen might imagine.

"Good. You should let him win. It's his party, after all."

"Careen still there?"

"Nah. She left a while ago. She decided to hit The Tavern."

"And you didn't?" He was relieved. Chances are, Dave would be at The Tavern. He never liked it when Jen was anywhere near that jerk.

"I figured I'd just wait around for you to get home," she said lazily. "I'm watching reruns."

"Don't wait up, Jen. I'm going to be really late."

"Oh," Jen said. "Well, you can wake me when you come in, if you want."

"'Kay. Good night," Jesse said quickly. He got ready to turn off the phone, relieved that he'd managed to get through the conversation without getting caught. But before he could press the red button on his cell, the firehouse door swung open. Mark, Artie's drunken law school bud, screamed out to him, "Jesse, man, you got to get in here. The girls are dancing with the fire poles. Those poles have never experienced anything like this, I'll tell you that."

Jesse gulped. He hoped Jen hadn't heard that.

No such luck. Suddenly, the voice on the other end of the phone sounded very cold and distant. "On second thought, Jesse, don't bother waking me when you come home. In fact, you might not want to bother coming home at all!" And then she slammed down the phone.

I HATE MEN! ALL MEN! THEY'RE SEXIST, LYING FREAKAZOIDS! IN FACT, JESSE IS THE KING FREAKAZOID!

I thought my husband was different. I thought he respected women. I thought he considered them equals—not people to be ogled, and even worse, for money. But I was wrong. Turns out Jesse's just like the rest of them. I can't believe he hired strippers for Artie's bachelor party—especially after he promised me he wouldn't!

It's amazing. You can share an apartment with a guy for almost a year and never really know him at all. I would have bet every penny I had that Jesse would never lie to me. Good thing I didn't. I'd be even more broke than I already am.

Well, we're probably going to be broke,

anyway, considering Jesse probably spent a lot of money hiring the "entertainment" for the party tonight. Imagine, he gives me crap about buying a couple of cheap pocketbooks, but he can spend a fortune on cheap women. Yeah, like that's real fair!

It's not even the strippers I'm the most mad about. It's the lying. I mean, if I can't trust Jesse, then what do we really have?

God. That's a scary thought.

—Jen

The Honeymoon Is Over

"Would you hurry up!" Jesse screamed into the bathroom.

"Relax. We've got tons of time. These things never start when the invitations say they will."

"I can't risk that," Jesse called back to her. "I'm the best man, remember? It's kind of important that I be there. People are liable to notice if there's a big hole standing next to Artie when the ceremony starts."

"Jesse, this day isn't about you," Jen called back to him. "You're not the one everyone's coming to see this time." Her tone was slightly cold and exhausted, much the same as it had been all week, since Jesse had arrived home after Artie's bachelor party. The fact that Jesse had lied to her had caused a real rift in their relationship. Not that Jesse had taken the accusation lying down. He'd reminded Jen that he wouldn't have had to lie to her in the first place if she hadn't been so controlling about the bachelor party. Neither one of them had backed down, which had left the apartment with a bit of a chill lately.

"Well, someone has to be Artie's best man. And he just happened to have picked me. *His best friend.* So I have to be on time!"

"Chill, will ya? I'm almost ready. I just have to slip on my dress and shoes and I'm ready to roll."

"You're not *dressed* yet?" Jesse asked, incredulous. "You've got to be kidding."

"The *dress* is the least of it. My hair's done, my makeup's on, and my panty hose are pulled up without a run. That's the stuff that takes up all the time. Boy, you'd think after nine months of being married to me you'd have figured that out by now."

"After nine months of being married to you, the only thing I've figured out is that you're always late!"

"I'm not always late," Jen argued, stepping

out of the bathroom as she struggled to zip her black strapless cocktail dress. "You're always *early*."

"I'm not early. I'm on time. I'm *always* on time. And I can prove it."

"Oh, I'm sure you can," Jen shot back. "All you have to do is pull out one of your seven gazillion watches and . . ."

"Gazillion is not a number," Jesse reminded her.

"Whatever," Jen groaned, sighing as she slipped on her shoes. "You should know, *Businessman*!" She spit the words out like venom. "It's amazing to me that you can be such a precision freak when it comes to things like your watches, or how long your perfect sideburns are, but you're a slob when it comes to your dirty underwear. The bathroom door is three feet from the hamper, yet you seem to think the doorknob is the perfect place to throw your dirty tidy whities when you head into the shower."

"Oh, is that what that thing is? A shower?" Jesse asked angrily. "I thought it was a jungle."

"A what?"

"A jungle. I figured that's what it must be

since I seem to have to make my way through all those pairs of panty hose hanging down to get to the thing." He moved his hands in front of his face like a hiker in a rain forest trying to push away hanging vines.

"I *dry* my panty hose in there," she explained. "Of course, I could just throw them out when they get dirty, like a normal person. But they cost two dollars a pair. Replacing them might send us to the poorhouse."

"Haven't you noticed?" Jesse asked her as he headed out the door. "We're already in the poorhouse. You ran up so many minutes on your cell phone last month, we went completely off our budget."

"There's that word again," Jen said through gritted teeth as she followed him down the stairs and out of the building.

"Budget!" Jesse shouted out at her. "Budget! Budget! Budget!" A woman passing by stared at him strangely. Jesse blushed slightly. He'd been so angry, he'd forgotten they were in the street.

Jen laughed haughtily, knowing how Jesse hated scenes. "Well, FYI, I ran up those minutes talking to *your* mother. She wanted to know what kind of sweater to get you: brown to match your eyes, or blue to go with your tan cords, or—God! That woman called me from half the malls in New Jersey."

"Oh great, thanks for blowing my birthday surprise!" Jesse yelled at her. He opened the car door on both sides and hopped into the driver's seat.

"Ooh, big surprise," Jen harrumphed, climbing into her seat. "A sweater. Now there's a shocker."

"Hey, you got me a sweater for Christmas."

"I didn't *get* you a sweater, I knitted you a sweater. There's a huge difference."

Jesse couldn't argue with that. So instead, he retorted by announcing, "Yeah, well, you fart in your sleep."

"What?"

"I said, YOU FART IN YOUR SLEEP." He repeated it loudly and slowly, as though he were trying to get through to someone who didn't speak any English.

"I do not."

"Oh yeah, you do. And it's gross. Not to mention very annoying."

"It can't be any more annoying than the way you snore," Jen countered, letting out a series of loud snorts and snores.

"Yeah, right. Like I really sound like that."

"Oh, you do," Jen assured him. "Trust me. I'm your wife. I'm there every night listening to the entire buzzsaw symphony."

"Well, that can't be any worse than what you do when I'm trying to tell a joke."

"What do I do?"

"How about giving out the entire punch line before I can. Sound familiar?"

"Well, maybe if you'd get a punch line right once in a while, I wouldn't have to do that for you. You screw up every joke! It's a good thing I didn't marry you for your sense of humor."

"Yeah, well what *did* you marry me for, then?" Jesse asked her pointedly.

"I can't remember, at the moment," Jen spat back angrily. She turned and faced the window. There was a knot in her stomach as she realized she really *couldn't* remember what it had been that had made her think she could spend the rest of her life with Jesse.

From the silence coming from his side of the car, it was obvious he was struggling with the same question.

Jen sat by herself in the third row of the church on the groom's side and waited for the wedding to begin. She hadn't really been sure where to sit. She definitely didn't consider herself a friend of the groom's, but she didn't know Felicia well enough to sit on her side of the church. So she'd settled for sitting on Artie's side. After all, her husband was the best man.

It was weird sitting in a church at a wedding. She hadn't been to a wedding since hers and Jesse's. This should have been a great experience—a time to do some reminiscing with Jesse about their own wedding day. Instead, she was sitting there, surrounded by people she didn't know from Artie's family and life, wondering why the hell she'd gotten married in the first place.

She watched as Jesse entered from the side of the room. Artie was by his side. For the first time since Jen had met him, Artie didn't look so confident. In fact, he looked downright petrified. He was sweating profusely from his forehead and wringing his hands. Jesse whispered something in his ear, and Artie shook his head, sending beads of sweat flying into the air.

He should *be nervous,* Jen thought ruefully. *The wedding's the easy part. If he were smart, he'd run the hell out of here as fast as those stubby legs can carry him. Escape, Artie. Escape before it's too late.*

Of course, Artie couldn't escape. There was a lot more than just a band of gold tying him to Felicia, after all. He was going to be a dad. That was a huge responsibility. No matter what happened between Felicia and himself, their lives were going to woven together one way or another, because they would have a child together. Jen's mind drifted back in time to her own pregnancy scare. At the time, she'd been disappointed about not being pregnant. But she and Jesse were in no position to raise a child. Hell, Jesse was behaving like a baby himself these days!

The music began and knocked all thoughts out of Jen's head for the moment. She watched as two adorable flower girls walked down the aisle, sprinkling rose petals in their paths. Then came Felicia's sisters, each dressed up in lavender ball gowns and shawls. Finally, Felicia herself started down the aisle, balancing nervously on her father's arm. Her face was ghostly pale, and her bouquet shook in her hands.

Jen wondered if she had looked that nervous on her wedding day. Probably not. She hadn't been particularly nervous walking down the aisle. In fact, she vaguely remembered she'd found the whole thing rather funny.

Maybe she *should* have been nervous—should have taken the whole thing a little more seriously. She and Jesse should have waited longer, till they knew each other better. Marriage shouldn't be a getting-to-know-you kind of venture. And yet, that was what she and Jesse had been doing these past nine months. Sure, some of it had been fun. But lately . . . well, lately, it wasn't fun at all. They seemed to do nothing but fight—over money, over whether to go to dinner at Adele and Sam's country club, over whether to invite Careen to come along with them to the movies, over whether Jesse should spend the morning playing golf with the guys in his department, over why Jen felt the need to talk to her mother three times a day, over why Jesse had to have all his clothes hanging in color and size order in the closet, over why Jen hadn't made the bed that morning . . .

Hell, lately, they fought over *everything*.

"If there is anyone here who can think of a reason why these two should not be joined in holy matrimony, let him speak now or forever hold his peace."

Jen's eyes met Jesse's as the minister spoke those words. Obviously, they were both having the same thoughts: *Stand up. Say something. Save these two from the mess they'd gotten themselves into.*

But they held their tongues. And after a moment, the minister declared those fateful words:

"By the power vested in me by the state of New Jersey, I now pronounce you husband and wife."

Jen sighed as she watched Artie kiss Felicia. *Husband and wife.* Poor things. That was a fate she wouldn't wish on anyone—not even on Artie.

Well, that was one hell of a wedding. Leave it to Artie to give his own toast at the reception. Good thing, though, since mine wasn't very uplifting. Just a lot of stuff about Artie as a frat boy, and how lucky he was to have a girl like Felicia and all that crap. Nothing particularly clever or original. I just couldn't seem to muster a whole lot of enthusiasm. Let's face it:

It's hard to be happy for someone else's wedded bliss when your own marriage is turning out to be a complete disaster.

I don't know what Jen's problem is lately. She's been on my case about everything. Nothing seems to make her happy. Miss "Never Go to Bed Angry" hasn't missed one night of yelling at me as soon as I turn out the lights. She's driving me crazy. Take last Thursday, for instance. I had to work late on a project that was due out by Friday at five to make the overnight mail collection. I told her I was going to pull an all-nighter at the office. She must have called my office ten times that night. Not because she wanted to talk to me, or because she missed me. No, Jen called to make sure I wasn't lying to her about working. Jeez. What does she want from me? I've apologized up, down, and sideways about Artie's party. Not that I'm really all that sorry. The guy deserved the kind of party he wanted, and I gave it to him. If Jen had been a more reasonable kind of wife, I wouldn't have had to lie. But no. I married the ultimate control freak. Everything has to be her way or the highway. I should have known that the minute she took down my vintage Beatles poster and replaced it with that hideous piece of art—and I use the word loosely—of Careen's. Oh, did I mention that we've been blessed with another lovely piece by Careen? She made it for my birthday. It's real special—it's a portrait of me (my face is painted in shades of magenta and chartreuse) surrounded by a collage made of all sorts of numbers cut from magazines and newspapers, a Jersey Devils ice-hockey team patch, and a photograph of my butt that she must have taken when I wasn't looking.

Somehow I don't think it was meant as a compliment.

All the same, Jen absolutely adored it, and insisted we hang it in our bedroom, where I get to stare at this thing every night before we have our evening argument and go to bed.

Speaking of bed, looking at my watch, it's already 11:00. And it seems we're just about ready for another round. I'd better get ready to defend myself against things I did six months ago, things I did today, and things *that Jen's certain I'm going to do in the future.*

Should be a blast. :(

Better run.

—Jesse

Until Death Do Us Part . . .
But Why Wait?

I guess this is the last you'll be hearing from me. Jesse and I have decided to call it quits. There wasn't any last boom, or final blow out. We both just know in our hearts that we're growing in opposite directions. Better to end things now. The more we hold on to the marriage, the harder it's going to be. Not that I can imagine things getting any harder than they are now.

I hate to admit it, but my mom was right. Jesse and I were just too damn young to get married. Learning to spend your life with another person is difficult enough under the best of circumstances, but doing it when you have so little money, and when you are at completely

*different stages in your life, is just a recipe for
disaster.*

*So here's my advice to all of you out there.
Don't stop looking for the love of your life. Just
don't rush into marriage when you find him.
Take the time to get to know each other. Take
lots of time. Lots and lots of time. Because
you're bound to discover that once the bloom
is off the rose, there are a lot of thorns underneath.*

Good luck!
—Jen

Jen sat back in the chair in Careen's dorm room
and pushed the Send button. She watched as
the screen flickered for a moment, went blank,
and then revealed the words "message sent."

And that was it. The last thing she had to do
that day. Day? No. It was dinnertime by now.
She'd spent most of the day dividing up stuff in
the apartment, and carting her few belongings
over to the dorms. She'd left Jesse with all that
awful La Chien furniture—there wasn't room
for it in the tiny senior suite, and frankly, even
after she got a place of her own, Jen wasn't
going to want that stuff. All she'd taken were

her clothes, the CDs she'd bought before the marriage, and Careen's *J-Squared* painting.

The painting had been dropped off at Jen's parents' house and placed in her old room. Jen hadn't exactly told her parents about her and Jesse yet. She'd simply said that she wanted to store the painting there for a while. She wasn't ready to hear her mother's "I told you so" speech any more than she was willing to look at the painting of her and Jesse. She hoped that someday she'd be able to look at it without crying.

Unfortunately this wasn't *that* day. Tears were already welling up in her eyes again just thinking about it.

She took a deep breath. *Start a conversation about something,* she urged herself. *Anything that isn't about him. Distract yourself.* "Are you sure it's okay with Liana if I stay in your dorm room?" she asked Careen, finally. "I mean, I could be here for at least two weeks."

"Sure. Liana has a boyfriend at Rutgers and she stays with him most nights, anyhow. Don't worry about it. Stay as long as you want."

"It's just till I can get something from student housing," Jen assured her. "It's hard to find something so late in the semester, but all I need is a bed somewhere. I don't even care if it's in a *freshmen* dorm."

Careen shuddered. "Freshmen? Ugh. Let's not go crazy, here, 'kay?"

"Oh, what's the big deal? There's not much time left before graduation, anyway."

"Don't remind me," Careen said, and gulped. "It's such a scary thought. No more student loans. No more dorm. I'll have to find an apartment, buy my own food. Hell, I might actually have to get a day job."

"You sound like you've been talking to Jesse," Jen murmured with more than a little sadness in her tone.

"Hey, his name's off-limits, remember?" Careen said, reminding Jen of their agreement. "History. In the past. You're moving on."

"Careen, that's not so easy. I only moved out of the apartment a few hours ago. It's going to take time to accept that things are really over, y'know."

Suddenly a loud *beep* came from Jen's laptop. "Oh, I've got an e-mail," she said aloud, turning her attention to the mailbox icon in the corner of the screen.

♥

Jennifer, Darling,

Everyone here is just absolutely devastated about what's happened to you and Jesse. We really should meet for lunch and talk. Are you free tomorrow? If not, let me know when's a good time for you.

—Sonja

"Who's Sonja?" Careen asked as she read the note over Jen's shoulder.

"She's the woman from Duets who set up our wedding contest."

Careen laughed. "Oh, the one with the exquisite taste who picked out my gown and the disco-themed centerpieces?"

"No. I think that was a wedding planner. Sonja's a businesswoman. She handles marketing and promotion."

"A *businesswoman*." Careen wrinkled her nose disdainfully. "Haven't you had enough of those types?"

"Come on, you can't just dismiss a whole group of people because of what they do for a living," Jen replied. "There are plenty of intelligent, creative people in the business world. We need them. Think about it. If artists didn't have managers and accountants, they'd actually have to read and understand their own contracts. They'd have to do their own publicity and taxes and—"

"Oh, this is so sad," Careen moaned.

"What."

"You lived with he-whose-name-we-will-not-say for far too long."

"What are you talking about?"

"Jen, you sound just like him." She sighed heavily and shook her head. "How long do you think it will take you to shake him?"

Jen sighed. She had a feeling Jesse would be with her—at least in spirit— for the rest of her life.

"It's so disheartening," Artie said as he poured another beer out of the pitcher. "I really thought you and Jen might be the ultimate married couple—except for Felicia and me, of course."

"Oh, of course," Jesse murmured, taking a big swig from his glass. "Actually, I think you were the one who warned me to not marry her. You said she was a flake."

"And I wasn't entirely incorrect," Artie replied. He sounded almost triumphant.

"You don't have to act so happy about it."

"Oh, I'm not happy. But I *am* your best friend. And as such, I'm about to make you an offer you can't refuse."

"What are you, Tony Soprano now?"

"No. I'm just the guy who's going to handle your divorce for free."

Jesse gulped. *Divorce.* He'd been avoiding the word ever since he and Jen had decided to end things. It was such an ugly word. It sounded harsh, and foreign. Angry. *Which, of course, is what it was all about.*

"I'm not quite there yet, Artie," Jesse said finally. "Jen and I just split up. I need a little time to sort things out. . . ."

"Hey, I understand your need to mourn the demise of your relationship," Artie said, trying his best to sound compassionate—and failing miserably. "But this is something you're going to have to do. And there's more to a dissolution of a marriage than you think. Division of property, and . . ."

"What property? All we had was some furniture, a few posters, and a couple of paintings by Careen. I took the one Careen made for me, and Jen took the big one. Not that I ever plan on taking mine out of hiding. But Jen insisted I take it and—"

"You just gave her the big one?" Artie interrupted. "You see, if you'd asked for my counsel, I would have advised you to keep them both as an investment. Or at least keep the larger one. Should Careen ever become famous . . ."

"Fat chance," Jesse said. "Besides, buying art as an investment is really shallow, Artie. It's supposed to fill your soul, not your bank account."

"See, now you're sounding like her," Artie said disdainfully. "Good thing you got out before she totally brainwashed you."

Jesse sighed. Artie would never understand just how much of Jen was in him . . . *would probably always be in him.*

"The thing is," Artie continued, "if you could just decide to file for divorce by the end of this semester . . ."

"What?"

"It's just that I need a project for my uncontested-divorce seminar and . . ."

Jesse's eyes burst open. "You want me to be your project?" he demanded.

"Well, hey, let's just say we'll be helping each

other out. I mean, you'll need a lawyer, and—"

"What I need is a new best friend," Jesse declared. He stood up, lifted his glass, and promptly poured what was left of his beer onto Artie's head. "See you around," he added, as he stormed out of the bar.

Jen,

We really need to talk. This all has come on so sudden, and there are things we never considered, or really talked about. I don't just mean between you and me personally, but there are legal things we have to work out and I think we should probably discuss

Jesse sat there for a moment, alone in the darkness of the apartment, and stared at the screen of his computer.

No. He definitely wasn't ready to think about any of that just yet. Damn Artie for even putting the idea in his head. Only Artie could have turned this whole thing into a business. *Division of property. Dissolution of a marriage.* Those were sick, unfeeling terms.

And they weren't a reality Jesse wanted to deal with. He reached down and, with a touch of a single button, erased the whole message. It was gone in a flash. As though it had never happened.

How ironic.

I'll Be the One in the Red Dress

Jen walked into the small sushi restaurant just off of the UNJ campus and looked around the room. Despite the dark lighting and closely packed tables of diners, she saw Sonja right away. She was hard to miss: tall, model-thin, with close-cropped dark hair and perfect make-up. She was wearing a green suit with a scarf tied around her neck. She looked like the poster woman for what a successful marketing executive should be. Jen laughed to herself, thinking what Careen would make of that.

"Hi, Sonja," Jen greeted her. She sat down in the seat across from the Duets executive.

Sonja looked up from her drink menu and studied Jen's weary face. "Jennifer, *darling*, how are you?" she asked with what seemed to be genuine concern. "You look a little tired. Still beautiful, but tired."

"It's midterms," Jen said quietly. "And everything else, I guess."

"It must be awful," Sonja acknowledged with just the right amount of sympathy. Then she smiled and tried to give her voice a more upbeat tone. "Have a seat. Get a drink. Maybe a warm sake. That's what I'm in the mood for. And look at this yummy menu. The sushi-sashimi lunch looks good. So does the dragon roll. Or you can mix and match things from the à la carte menu. Oh, aren't you a vegetarian? Well, there are plenty of veggie rolls for you, and they make the most delicious seaweed salad. Go ahead. Order anything you want. It's all on Duets."

"Wow. Thanks, Sonja. It's been a while since I had sushi. It's so expensive, and Jesse and I don't have . . . I mean, we never *had* any money and . . ."

"No need to explain, darling. I remember what it was like to be a starving college student. That's why I chose sushi. It's not exactly something they serve in the dorm cafeteria—unless you count those awful pieces of California roll they sometimes put in the salad bar."

"Exactly," Jen said, and nodded. "And the rice is always hard as a rock in those."

Sonja laughed, and turned her attention back to the menu. Jen scanned her own menu as well, grateful for the few minutes of silence before she and Sonja really got down to talking. She had no doubt that Sonja would want to know the details of what had happened between her and Jesse. Jen kind of figured she owed her at least some information, especially after all the things Duets had done for them with the wedding and the furniture and all.

Sure enough, as soon the waitress had taken their order, Sonja turned the conversation toward more personal things. "So, you and Jesse are really over?"

Jen shrugged dejectedly. "It was . . . I don't know. I guess we made a mistake rushing in like that. We didn't know anything about each other. And we just aren't in the same place right now."

"Maybe you shouldn't make any final decisions right now. You're in the middle of midterms, and Jesse's not even in his job a year. You've both been under so much pressure. Have you thought about couples therapy? I could recommend a good doctor who could meet with you both."

Jen sighed. "It won't help. There's no way any doctor could fix this mess. Jesse and I just have irrevocable . . . irrec . . . oh, what's the word?"

"You mean irreconcilable differences?" Sonja asked.

Jen nodded. "That's it."

"My first husband and I used that one in our divorce," Sonja told her.

"Oh, you were married?"

"Three times. But I'm single now," Sonja replied matter-of-factly as she poured some hot sake from her little white pitcher.

"You've been divorced *three times* and you can still work for a company like *Duets*?" Jen was positively incredulous.

Sonja laughed. "I guess I'm just a hopeless romantic. I'm convinced that sooner or later I'll meet Mr. Right."

"I thought I had," Jen admitted as she took a sip of her diet cola. She'd been careful not to order the sake. These days, all alcohol did was put her on a crying jag. "But now I think that's all just a bunch of bull."

"That's because you're coming off a relationship," Sonja told her knowingly. "What you need is to jump right back into the dating pool and start again. You'll see. There's someone for everyone."

"Maybe," Jen said slowly. "In a couple months, or a year. Right now I need to—"

Sonja sighed heavily. "Jen . . . ," she interrupted her. "The thing is . . . you sort of have to get back into dating now."

Jen shook her head. "Thanks for the advice, but I'm just not ready. Gosh, we've only been separated a little more than a week."

"Jennifer, this is more than advice," Sonja said, her voice suddenly losing its friendly sound and becoming more businesslike. "This is business. You have to continue dating. And you have to do it through Duets."

"Why?"

"You have three more months left on your contract to us. And frankly, a broken marriage isn't exactly the image we want to leave our customers with. You need to start going through our listings and begin dating again, and make it sound as though you're actually having fun."

"But—"

"There are no *buts*," Sonja assured her. "This is

what you have to do. Unless, of course, you want to begin paying us back for that entire wedding. You'll need fifteen thousand dollars. . . ."

"FIFTEEN THOUSAND DOLLARS!" Jen's voice rang out across the restaurant. Some of the other patrons stopped and stared in her direction. She blushed and lowered her head.

"Yes," Sonja replied quietly, seemingly nonplussed by Jen's outburst. "And that's just your half. We've invested a lot of money in you and Jesse. And we aren't going to let you give our business a bad name. You've got to show our members that even after something as traumatic as you've been through, you're able to trust us to get you back on the right track." She took another sip of her sake. "It's not the marketing campaign we'd bargained for, but you can never predict what happens with these things. All you can do is be ready with a little damage control when the emergencies pop up."

These things. Damage control. Jen took a deep breath. She was seeing Sonja for what she really was for the very first time, and it was not a pretty picture. Apparently, she and Jesse were nothing but business items to this woman. Players on a chessboard that she moved around to make sure she stayed in the game. Sure, Sonja had *pretended* to care about them, with all her "Jesse dears," and "Jennifer darlings," but she hadn't cared a bit. At least not about anyone except herself and her career.

"Have you already talked to Jesse about this?" Jen asked slowly.

Sonja nodded. "Of course."

"And he's agreed to start dating again?"

Sonja took another sip of her sake. "Jesse is a wise man. He knows there's nothing else he can do. He's already sent in his ad. In fact, he seemed to be quite interested in finding out who was going to answer."

Jennifer blinked her eyes. Suddenly she felt light-headed. The room began to spin.

Sonja noticed the change in her expression. "Honestly, Jennifer, don't take this all so personally. It's just business," she advised.

Jen frowned. "Not personal? You ask me to start dating one week after I break up with my husband, and you say it's not personal? Hell, your whole damn company is *built* on personals. Don't you see that?"

"I don't know why you're making such a fuss. Jesse wasn't like this at all. "

The thought that Jesse could have no trouble just jumping back into the dating pool—no matter what the reason—really began to piss Jen off. The day they'd decided to split up, Jen had called him a worm. But she'd overestimated him—and done the entire worm population a disservice. "Business is the *only* thing Jesse understands," she said between gritted teeth.

"Maybe. But he certainly understands that he doesn't want to be sued for fifteen thousand dollars. That could destroy a person's credit rating forever," Sonja explained calmly.

Jen was trapped, and she knew it. There was no escaping the prison that was Duets. "Fine," she said quietly. "I'll do whatever you want."

Sonja smiled triumphantly, seeming not to see the sudden green pallor that had taken over Jen's face. She looked toward the kitchen and exclaimed, "Oh, goody. Here comes lunch. I can't wait to dive into that eel!"

"Here's one that doesn't sound too creepy," Careen suggested that evening when Jen returned to the dorms after her ill-fated lunch with Sonja. Surprisingly, Careen hadn't thought Sonja's idea was so bad. In fact, she'd even offered to look over some potential dating partners for Jen.

"'Do you like piña coladas, and taking walks in the rain?'" Jen read aloud. "Oh, no."

"You like both of those," Careen reminded her.

"Yeah, but I never liked the song."

Careen looked confused. She scanned the ad. "Song? What song? He doesn't mention any song."

"These are lyrics from a really bad seventies song about personal ads," Jen explained, pointing at the screen. "So either this guy is as old as my father, or he's got really crappy taste in retro music. Either way, he's not my type."

"Well, if you're going to be picky." Careen scanned the page. "Okay, here's another one."

My friends actually suggested I put an ad on this site. I'm kind of shy, and not likely to just go up to a girl on my own. I'm kind of inexperienced at that sort of thing. If you're the kind of girl who doesn't mind quiet evenings, going to the movies, reading books in front of the fire, and staying away from the party scene, then maybe we should meet. . . .

❤

Careen stopped there. "Never mind. This guy sounds like a dud."

"No he doesn't," Jen said. "He sounds kind of sweet. Besides, I'm not exactly in a partying mood these days." She pushed Careen out of the way and began to type in the response box.

Hi. I read your ad. You sound very nice. Maybe we can meet for coffee at The Beanery on the UNJ campus, on Friday at 3. If you decide to come, look for me. I'll be the one in the red dress.

By Friday afternoon, Jen had three times almost chickened out of meeting the guy who'd posted the ad on Duets. But a very persuasive call from Sonja had finally hastened her out of the door and sent her on the way to The Beanery, dressed in a long, flowing, Indian-style red gauzy dress. She'd tied her hair up in a ponytail and had not bothered with makeup. It wasn't exactly the way Jen would have ordinarily dressed for a date, but she didn't actually consider this a date. To her, it was more of a business obligation.

As she sat at a small table in the corner, sipping her peppermint latte, she wondered what Jesse was doing right now. According to Sonja, he'd already gone on two dates—and had posted his feelings about them on Duets' Web site. Jen had been tempted to call up his letters, but she'd decided not to. The thought that Jesse was starting up again in the singles scene without even looking back was just too upsetting to her. Reading about his dates would be too much.

"Excuse me, are you Jennifer?" a tall, muscular guy with short dark hair and green eyes interrupted her.

Jen looked up, surprised. If this was the guy from Duets, he certainly didn't look anything like she'd expected. Somehow, she'd pictured a skinny, bookish kind of guy—sort of like Adam Brody on the *O.C.* "Yes, I'm Jennifer," she said quietly.

"I'm Charles," the guy announced in a loud, deep voice as he took the seat across from her. "I'm the one who posted the ad."

"Oh." She put her hand out. "It's nice to meet you."

"That's no way to say hello," Charles told her. He grabbed her hand, reached across the table, and kissed her on both cheeks. Then he leaned back lazily in his chair and stared at her in a way that made Jen blush.

"Well," she said, "you sure don't seem like a shy guy, Charlie."

"That's *Charles*," he told her.

"Sorry."

"No problem, it happens all the time." Charles raised his hand in the air and called over the waitress. "Sweetheart, could you get me a large coffee, heavy on the cream?" he asked her with a wink.

The waitress, like Jen, blushed as he spoke to her. There was something about this guy that made everything he said or did seem like it had another, *sleazier*, meaning.

"Um, sure," the waitress murmured in response.

"Gee, you don't really seem shy," Jen told him honestly as the waitress walked away.

"I don't?"

"Not at all. You're nothing like the way you described yourself."

Charles laughed. "Well, I'll let you in on a little secret, Jenny. . . ."

"Jennifer." *Two could play at this game.*

"Whatever. Anyway, the secret is, I'm not shy at all. I just wrote that so someone as cute as you would answer my ad."

Jen was shocked at his honesty, even if she didn't understand what he was talking about.

"It's simple psychology," Charles continued. "Somehow, the cute girls all want to date a shy, sensitive guy. So I figure if I want to meet cute girls, I have to make them figure they're helping out a poor, inexperienced soul. It really works. You're the third girl to answer my ad this week."

"Oh," Jen replied. "How interesting. Are you going out with any of them again?"

"Probably. I'm just waiting for them to call me back. In the meantime, I thought I'd meet you. And I'm glad I did." He took her hand in his. "Aren't you feeling the electricity here?"

"Oh, I'm feeling something," Jen said sarcastically.

"Great. Now I know I spent my money wisely by posting that ad."

"But why bother with Duets?" Jen asked. "A guy like you doesn't seem to have any trouble talking to girls."

"I know," Charles agreed. "But it's the strangest thing. You're not going to believe this, but it's not always easy for me to get dates. Sometimes the girls actually say no." He flexed an arm muscle and checked his reflection in the window. "I guess they're intimidated by the way I look or something. But hey. This is the kind of body you get when you teach at a gym."

"Oh, you teach?"

"Yeah, I train businesspeople who come after work. They put in their time on the treadmill or the weight machines, and head over to the juice bar to make connections. Me, I'm not into that nine-to-five thing. I just like working out. Enjoying life."

"Mm. Interesting," Jen murmured, wondering—*hoping*—that Jesse was having just as lousy a time on his dates as she was right now.

Jen's hopes were well founded. At the moment, Jesse found himself seated across the table from Lucy Willis, a business major at the University of New Jersey. She was a graduating senior who was currently interning at a big accounting firm in the city.

"So, I think we should probably split this check," Lucy said in a very businesslike manner. "That way, there's no obligation on either side."

"Fine," Jesse agreed. "Although I'll pay, if you want."

"No, that won't be necessary. I have a paying internship. Besides, I'm not in the mood for a date that's full of power plays. I don't feel like struggling to see who'll wind up on top."

Jesse smirked, thinking about what Jen would have made out of a line like that. She'd most certainly have let out a good laugh—that bell-like laugh that . . .

No. Jesse stopped himself. He had to stop thinking about her. It was making him crazy. "So, what do you do for fun?"

"I play squash at the New York Health and Racquet Club."

"Cool. I've played a little squash myself."

"Really," Lucy replied as she picked up a knife and fork and began cutting her slice of pizza into tiny pieces. "We should play sometime. But I have to warn you that I played competitively in high school. I'm very good."

"Your high school had a squash team?"

"Of course," she replied. "Most of the better private schools do. And of course I was also on the fencing team. That helped me get into UNJ early decision. They look for things like that. What sports do you play?"

"I'm into skating."

"Oh. Hockey? "

"Sometimes, in pickup games. But mostly I just skate. You know figure eights, a few jumps . . ."

"Oh." Lucy frowned as she put another forkful of pizza in her mouth. "How do you win at that?"

"I don't compete," Jesse told her. "I just like to move around on the ice. It feels so free."

"Oh." Lucy's interest seemed to be waning.

"You don't like to feel free?" Jesse asked her.

"I prefer to be in control. You succeed better that way."

Jesse frowned. "I suppose that depends on your definition of success," he suggested.

"Well, a corner office and a starting salary in the high five figures would be a start," Lucy said, smiling. "You know, here it is April already, and I'm still negotiating for the best job offer. You wouldn't believe the kind of lowballing some of these firms are trying to get away with. But I'm not concerned. Graduation is still two months away. And I've got it all under control."

Jesse nodded, wondering how this control freak would feel if she knew she had a big piece of broccoli stuck between her teeth. The fact that Jesse knew it and she didn't suddenly made him feel extremely powerful.

Sitting there at the table with Lucy also made him feel extremely lonesome. Somehow he couldn't believe he was dating again. He'd thought that was all behind him.

But the fact that Jesse *was* dating wasn't the most depressing part of it all. No. The worst part was that he knew Jen was dating too. The thought of her out with another guy was tying him up in knots.

Haven't I Seen You Somewhere Before?

Jesse buttoned up his leather jacket as he walked down the block. He couldn't believe it was almost Halloween. The time had just sort of flown by. He wasn't sure how. It wasn't like he'd been busy with a whirlwind of events or anything. In fact, he hadn't been doing much, other than working and working out. Life had just sort of fallen into a rut.

The contract with Duets had finally ended in August—right around the time of what would have been his anniversary with Jen. After that, Sonja stopped calling and constantly reminding him that Jen was dating a myriad of men. Without that to make him angry—*jealous*—Jesse didn't find himself going out on a whole lot of dates. Sure, every now and then his mother or his sister-in-law would try to fix him up with the daughter of some friend, or a friend of a friend, but it never really led to much.

Tonight, he was pretty sure, was going to be yet another of those horrendous evenings. Perfect Megan had met what she'd described as "the girl of Jesse's dreams" and wanted to set them up on a blind date. Jesse had protested, and refused to call for weeks now. But Megan had been very persistent. So Jesse had phoned the girl, Ashley, as much to get Megan out of his hair as anything else.

At least Ashley *seemed* to have interests other than finding a husband and social climbing. She'd arranged for them to meet at a gallery opening in Hoboken. She'd gotten tickets from one of the clients at the travel agency where she worked. He figured if she worked at a travel agency, she must like traveling. That would give them something to talk about, anyway. Something he could never discuss with Jen, who hadn't traveled much. Maybe he could actually have a conversation that didn't remind him of something Jen had said or done.

Surprisingly, Jesse actually found himself

looking forward to the evening. Not necessarily the meeting-Ashley part—she'd sounded a little too giggly for his taste—but the idea of going to an art opening kind of intrigued him. This wouldn't be the first gallery he'd stopped into in the past few months. His business had been taking him to Jersey City from time to time, and there was a whole cluster of galleries there. He'd spent a lot of lunch hours just looking around, and he was actually beginning to understand some of the more way-out stuff. He'd wanted to call Jen and let her know about his new interests, but he'd never had the guts. She probably didn't want to hear from him, anyway. Still, he kept on going to galleries. There was something about being around artwork that made Jesse feel soothed and happy. It reminded him of better times—before he and Jen had started to fight. A sort of Paradise Lost.

"Jesse! Jesse! Over here!" a small redhead in a camel-hair trench coat stood in front of the gallery, waving wildly in his direction.

"You must be Ashley," he greeted her as he walked over.

"The one and only."

"How'd you recognize me?"

"Megan showed me a picture from last Thanksgiving. But I must say, you're better looking in person."

Last Thanksgiving. Jesse's mind drifted back. What a mess that day had been—between Jen's pregnancy scare, and that creepy Austin kid catching them in the tub. "I wasn't at my best that day," he told Ashley honestly.

"Oh. You must have been fighting with your ex. Megan told me all about her."

Jesse frowned. He could only imagine what Megan must have said. "Yeah, well, what do you say we go inside?" he said, changing the subject.

"Okay. I don't know how good this show's gonna be, though. It's a collection of three new up-and-coming artists. Some of their stuff could be a little whacked out."

Jesse laughed. "That's okay. I like new artists."

"If it stinks we can always go to dinner or something," Ashley suggested.

"Let's give it a chance," Jesse replied, surprising even himself by the fact that he actually meant it.

The gallery was crowded when they walked in. The group was mixed—some of the hippie-type crowd Jen used to hang with in her art history days were mingling among the better-dressed collectors. Everyone, however, seemed to be taking advantage of the buffet and bar that had been set up in the corner. The appeal of the free eats wasn't lost on Ashley. The food buffet was the first place she chose to examine.

"Want to try some of those hors d'oeuvres?" she asked Jesse.

Jesse was hungry, but one of the paintings had already caught his eye. "No, you go ahead. I want to get a better look at that piece over there."

Ashley followed the direction of his glance. "You mean that weird painting of a blue-faced woman with all the makeup brushes, Weight Watchers food labels, and hair-dye boxes glued around her?"

Jesse nodded. "I think I might know the artist."

"Wow. You know artists?" Ashley asked, impressed. "Cool. Do you think you could introduce me to one?"

"Sure. Why don't you go get some snacks and I'll see if I can find out if the woman I know actually did this one?"

As Ashley walked off, Jesse headed over to the collection of paint and collage pieces on the far wall. He didn't even have to check to see whose name was on the plaque. He already knew the art was by Careen. Surprisingly, he found himself *hoping* that she was at the opening. *Imagine being excited to see Careen.* But Jesse couldn't help himself. She was a link to a happier time.

"Well, if it isn't Numbers Boy," Careen said, suddenly coming up behind him.

Jesse knew the voice right away. He turned, and burst into laughter. Some things never changed. Careen was wilder than ever—this time, her hair was two-toned, black on one side and magenta on the other. She was wearing a skintight leather mini, and carrying a rather large drink—also magenta in color, with a little umbrella in it.

"Jesse Merriman, you're the last person I'd expect to see here."

"I'm, um, on a date," he said as explanation.

"Oh? An art lover? Maybe a collector?" Careen seemed interested.

"No, more like a free food lover." He turned and pointed to the buffet. "That's her, the one over by the cheese and crackers."

"Mmm. Cute." Careen laughed. "She's in the process of sneaking rolls into her pocketbook."

"Megan fixed us up. She thought we'd be perfect together."

Careen rolled her eyes. "And you're not?"

Jesse sighed. "Not exactly."

"So I gather you haven't met anyone special?"

Jesse shook his head. "No. I've been introduced to some nice people, but they're not . . . I mean they never are . . ."

"They never will be either," Careen assured him. "She's one of a kind."

Jesse paused, debating about whether to ask her if Jen was seeing anyone steadily, but he couldn't bring himself to do it. He didn't think he could handle it if she was. So instead, he changed the topic. "I guess you're doing okay. I mean, a show like this can be a pretty big deal."

Careen smiled. "Surprisingly, yes. There's actually a market for my work out there."

"I'm not surprised. It's art with a purpose and a vision. It's unique, and yet the messages are universal."

"Numbers Boy!" Careen exclaimed. "That was positively insightful."

"I've been looking around at things lately."

"Impressive," Careen admitted. "Anyway, I guess other people agree with you. I've sold a few pieces, and I have a show planned for a small museum in Colorado in a couple of weeks. Not that I'll be able to afford to fly out there to see it. And you're right. This gallery is a huge deal. Apparently, rich people are coming to Hoboken more often. It makes them feel artsy. Crossing the Hudson—taking a walk on the wild side." She laughed haughtily. "Mostly though, I'm temping. Gotta pay for oil paints and canvases."

Jesse nodded, imagining how many office filing systems Careen must have screwed up in the past few months of doing temporary work. But rather than razz her about working in offices, he decided to take the high road for a change. "The owners of this gallery considered *you* up-and-coming," he complimented her. "Jen always predicted that."

"Actually, in this case, I had a little 'in' with the management. My roommate works here." She turned slightly and looked toward the wall on the far side of the gallery.

Jesse's eyes flew open. He'd imagined this moment over and over again, each time he'd stepped into a gallery. But it was always just a daydream.

Tonight though, it was real. She was here. Sure, she'd cut her hair shorter, into some sort of French bob thing, and she'd lost a little weight, but those blue eyes were still dancing, her smile was still enchanting and . . .

Then suddenly, she opened her lips and let out a laugh. That bubbly, exciting laugh. A laugh that could only belong to Jen.

Careen stood there for a moment, watching his expression. Finally she took him by the arm and began dragging him across the room. "Come on," she said.

"What?"

"Against my better judgment, I'm introducing you to the assistant to the manager of the gallery."

"Wow. Assistant to the manager," Jesse was impressed.

"Yeah, she has a job," Careen said ruefully. "With benefits and a pension plan, and all that other stuff I know nothing about."

Jesse frowned. Obviously Jen had shared the details of some of their arguments with Careen. "No, I just meant I'm glad someone recognized how smart she is."

"Good catch." Careen laughed. "You're almost charming. Let's see if you can do as well when you're talking to her."

Talk to her? Jesse stomach did a flip, and his throat seemed to catch. He'd had this conversation a million times in his head. But now that he was going to actually have the opportunity to talk to Jen in person . . . "Hey, that's okay. She's already talking to that woman. And she probably doesn't want to see me, anyway."

"She shouldn't." Careen said bluntly. She stopped in her tracks. "You're right. Forget about talking to Jen. I can tell you'll have a much more stimulating conversation chatting with your date over there . . . if she can stop shoving pieces of quiche in her mouth long enough to talk."

Jesse sighed. Careen had a point. Jen *was* interesting to chat with. And they were adults. They could carry on a conversation like any two people who had once known each other.

Except they weren't any two people. They were Jen and Jesse. J-squared. And they had a lot of unfinished business to deal with. He flinched slightly, but let Careen drag him the rest of the way across the room.

"Jen, look what kind of riffraff is showing up at these places nowadays," Careen announced.

Jen looked up for a moment and gasped. She stared at him for a moment, unable to speak.

"Jen, aren't you going to introduce us?" A thirty-something woman in a black silk suit and pearls, probably a buyer, Jess figured, sidled up beside them. She smiled in Jesse's direction.

Jesse smiled back slightly.

"Oh, um . . . Marie, this is Jesse. He's my ex . . . well my *almost* ex . . ."

"These two just can't seem to sign those papers," Careen explained.

"Her ex? And you came to the opening, anyway?" the woman in the suit remarked to Jesse. "How incredibly civilized."

"Well, I didn't actually know that Jen . . . ," Jesse began.

Jen stared at him, seeming unable to believe that he was really there.

Careen stood there for a moment, watching the two of them watch each other. Finally, she took the woman in the black suit by the arm. "Marie, could you come with me for just a moment? There's a piece I've done that I think would be just perfect for the lobby of your office building."

As Marie and Careen walked off, Jesse and Jen stood frozen in place, unable to speak or move. Finally, it was Jen who broke the silence. "So what are you doing here?"

"I'm sort of on a date. . . ." Jesse regretted the words as soon as they left his mouth. Even more so after he saw the expression on Jen's face. "Megan fixed us up. It's a blind date . . . a real disaster," he added quickly.

"Perfect Megan strikes again." Jen sighed, remembering how crictical and uptight her former sister-in-law had been.

There was silence between them as they both wondered what to say next. Jesse frowned. A year ago he never would have imagined that they'd ever run out of things to talk about.

Again it was Jen who broke the silence, turning the conversation into something light and less uncomfortable. "Guess what? I actually have an office now."

"You're kidding."

"Okay, well, not an office. It's sort of a cubicle, actually. But it has a desk and a phone."

"I don't believe you."

"Come on, I'll show you." Jen took him by

the arm and began pulling him toward the back of the gallery.

"Shouldn't you be out here trying to mingle with buyers?"

Jen shook her head. "That's more William's job. He's the gallery owner. The rest of us are his minions. Actually my job is mostly a lot of assistant work. Getting coffee, making sure the shows are ready, making appointments for William to meet new artists. But I do get to help in creating the catalogs—you know, having slides made of the pieces, writing some of the little blurbs, getting everything to the designer in time."

Jesse thought back to the way Jen had flinched when he'd mentioned going into publishing. This wasn't so different. But an I-told-you-so wouldn't be the right thing to say right now. Instead, he silently followed her back into her cubicle.

The workspace was total Jen: Papers were piled up everywhere on her desk, there were stacks of slides on an extra chair, and she had two pairs of shoes hidden in the corner. There were also two posters on the wall—one of a painting by Kandinsky, the other a blown-up picture of the cover of Franz Kafka's book *The Metamorphosis*.

"So, what made you bring *your date* here?" Jen asked. She was trying to sound nonchalant, but the tone in her voice revealed her true feelings.

Jesse shrugged. "She got the passes from a client," he explained.

"Oh." Jen sounded disappointed. "I thought maybe you'd discovered modern art."

"Actually, I sorta have. I've been stopping into galleries from time to time, and I even visited the Museum of Modern Art once during that Picasso exhibit."

"Wow," Jen sounded genuinely impressed. "Picasso."

"Yeah."

"I saw that one too," Jen told him. "It was a fantastic exhibit. There were some of his little-known works there."

"Yeah." Jesse looked around the cubicle as the silence once again began to envelope them. Finally, the one question that had been nagging at him for months literally popped out of his mouth. "Jen, how come you started dating right away? Didn't you . . . I mean, didn't our marriage mean anything? Didn't you need time to . . ." He stopped mid-sentence, suddenly ashamed of just blurting out his thoughts like that.

She looked at him, astonished. "You've got a lot of nerve. You started dating right away too."

"Only because I was mad at you. When Sonja told me that you were actually *excited* at the idea of answering new ads, I figured there was no hope for us. So I—"

"Sonja told you I *wanted* to date?'"

"It's okay, Jen," Jesse assured her. "I've come to terms with it already."

"But she told me *you* were dating. You put an ad on the Duets site and everything. She said you'd already agreed to it because of our business deal."

Jesse looked at her, confused. "What would our business deal have to do with it?"

"Sonja told me that if I didn't keep writing to Duets, she could sue me for breach of contract."

"So what?"

"So that's why I started dating," Jen explained. "She told me I had to write about the dates."

"You didn't have to write about dates. That contract didn't stipulate *what* we had to write. Only that we *would* write. You could have written about anything."

Jen sat down on the one empty chair in her cubicle. "Oh my God." She sighed.

"All you had to do was call me. I would have explained it."

"I would never have called you," Jen said. "I was so angry that you were dating again that I . . ."

"Exactly. I felt so betrayed. Despite everything, I really thought we could work things out. I figured we just needed a little time apart to think. I had faith in us until—"

"Until Sonja butted in," Jen finished his thought. "That's how I felt, too, Jesse. I had faith. But I guess Sonja didn't have as much faith in us as we did."

"A woman who got divorced three times probably figured good-bye meant good-bye. She got us to start dating people from her site so she could minimize her losses."

"Boy, she really played us," Jen moaned. "I could kill her."

"Yeah well, too late now. We've been done

with Duets for a few months already," Jesse reminded her.

"It has been a long time," Jen said, studying Jesse's face.

He looked back at her, wondering if she was thinking the same thing he was. But there wasn't time to find out. Suddenly, a frantic little man in a gray suit came running back to the cubicle.

"Jennifer, there you are. I've been looking all over for you. There's a big collector who is interested in one of Careen's paintings. But I need you to be with her when she tries to explain the meaning of her work. We can't leave Careen alone with a collector. Heaven knows *what* she'll say."

Jesse laughed. Same old Careen.

"Don't worry William, I'm on my way," Jen assured her boss. She turned to Jesse. "Sorry," she added sincerely.

Jesse nodded, knowing that the word had so much more meaning than anyone would ever know. "So am I," he replied honestly. As Jen walked away, Jesse reached down onto her desk and grabbed one of her pale blue and white business cards.

Duet Again

Jen sat at her desk on Monday morning and stared at the catalog copy on her computer screen. This was always the hardest part of her job. Finding new artists that were intriguing and marketable wasn't the issue. But trying to use words to explain their pieces—now *that* was tough.

She glanced at her watch—a little silver bracelet-type of timepiece—and sighed. Ten thiry. Too early for lunch, too late for breakfast. But a coffee break . . . she grabbed the mug from her desk and started over toward the machine in the little kitchenette that was set up in the back of the gallery offices.

She was returning to her office with a big cup of java when she heard her computer let out a warning signal. She walked over to her desk and saw a little envelope flashing in the corner of her screen. Oh, goody. Someone had sent her an e-mail. Probably Careen with gossip about some of their friends. Careen was always blasting Jen with e-mails while she was at work.

Jen settled back in her chair and took a big gulp of her coffee as she opened the e-mail. But the note wasn't from Careen. Instead, an advertisement popped onto the screen.

Are you in the medical profession?
Male with injured heart and badly bruised ego seeks the help of a trained female professional who will be able to bandage him up and breathe new life into his painful existence. The perfect person for this job is someone with a winning sense of humor, a sense of what's really important in this life, and a desire to try again. The perfect applicant will share the patient's forgive-and-learn-from-the-past philosophy.

P.S. I've never stopped loving you.

Jen let out a bright, bubbly laugh and picked up the phone. Some things about Jesse would never change. Just like his very first Duets ad, this little note was funny and clever. Unique. Also kind of corny, even goofy. And maybe just a little uptight. Instinctively she began dialing Jesse's work number.

"Jesse Merriman."

Jen smiled. His voice never ceased to make her whole body tingle. "Hi. This is the love doctor," she teased.

"Oh, thank goodness," Jesse said. "I wasn't sure there was anyone out there who could help me."

"I don't know if I can help. But I'm willing to try."

"That's all I can ask," Jesse said. "What do you prescribe?"

"How about dinner tonight?" Jen suggested. "There's a little Thai place not far from where I work. It's quiet, and we can talk there."

"Good," Jesse said. "I think we need to talk. We have a lot of things to work out."

"Yeah, but I think there's hope," Jen told him quietly.

"For me?"

"For us," Jen assured him. "For both of us."

"J-squared," Jesse replied.

"Mm-hmm," Jen agreed. "The perfect *duet*."

She stopped for a minute. "Okay, maybe not perfect," she admitted.

"But never boring," Jesse told her. He paused for a minute. "I meant it, Jen. That thing about having never stopped loving you. I really meant it."

"I know you did," she told him. "I didn't stop loving you either. But it's going to take more than that."

"I agree," Jesse said. "But this time, I'm willing to work at it. To compromise. I'm determined to have things go right, Jen. Just tell me what you need me to do."

"Start by being on time for dinner," Jen teased him. "Seven sharp. And I'll know if you're late. I'm wearing a watch these days." Then she let out that wonderful laugh again.

"All right." Jesse laughed along with her. "I'll be on time, I promise. Do you maybe want to go somewhere after, for dessert? Like this bakery I saw the other night?"

Jen took a deep breath. They were speaking so easily now. Like old times—well, sort of like old times. Back then they didn't always spend a whole lot of time on conversation. They seemed to have better things to do with their mouths. A familiar longing began to take over her. She'd missed him so much. And now . . . well, now she really wanted to be near him again. Forever. Really forever, this time. Which meant that no matter how attracted to him she might be feeling physically, they had to take it slow. Not hurry into things. That was where they'd messed up before. "You know what Jesse, let's wait and see how dinner goes," she said gently.

"Okay, Jen," Jesse agreed. "Whatever you say."

"Remember that phrase," she teased. "It just might come in handy in the future."

"Fine with me. As long as there is a future," Jesse told her.

"I think there is," Jen replied sincerely. "And for the first time in a long time, I'm looking forward to it."

Nancy Krulik is the author of more than 150 books for children and young adults, including the *New York Times* best-seller *Leonoardo DiCaprio: A Biography*, and two other Simon Pulse novels, *Ripped at the Seams* and *Love & Sk8*. She lives in Manhattan with her husband, composer Daniel Burwasser, and their two children. Although Nancy and her husband are way past the official newlywed stage, they still try to go on as many honeymoons as possible.

As many as 1 in 3 Americans
who have HIV... don't know it.

TAKE CONTROL.
KNOW YOUR STATUS.
GET TESTED.

To learn more about HIV testing,
or get a free guide to HIV and
other sexually transmitted diseases:

www.knowhivaids.org
1-866-344-KNOW

Jeremy Iversen

21 The age at which freedom rings
The number of drinks consumed in one night

**The honest new novel about the
greatest day in a college kid's life**

PUBLISHED BY SIMON PULSE

❀ WANTED ❀

Single Teen Reader in search of a FUN romantic comedy read!

How Not to Spend Your Senior Year
BY CAMERON DOKEY

Royally Jacked
BY NIKI BURNHAM

Ripped at the Seams
BY NANCY KRULIK

Cupidity
BY CAROLINE GOODE

Spin Control
BY NIKI BURNHAM

South Beach Sizzle
BY SUZANNE WEYN & DIANA GONZALEZ

★ *Available from Simon Pulse* ★
✱ *Published by Simon & Schuster* ✱